ESCAPE 2 AFRICA™

HarperCollins®, ☰®, and HarperEntertainment
are trademarks of HarperCollins Publishers.
Madagascar: Escape 2 Africa: The Junior Novel
Madagascar: Escape 2 Africa ™ & © 2008 DreamWorks Animation L.L.C.
Printed in the United States of America. All rights reserved.
For information address HarperCollins Children's Books,
a division of HarperCollins Publishers,
1350 Avenue of the Americas, New York, NY 10019.
www.harpercollinschildrens.com
Library of Congress catalog card number: 2008930194
ISBN 978-0-06-144783-9
Book design by John Sazaklis
❖
First edition

# MADAGASCAR
## ESCAPE 2 AFRICA™

# THE JUNIOR NOVEL

Adapted by
J. E. Bright

**HarperEntertainment**
*An Imprint of HarperCollins Publishers*

# PROLOGUE

**O**n the wild African savanna, an adorable baby lion named Alakay frolicked in the tawny grass.

Far behind him, a mountainous volcano poked up into the clouds. In the middle distance, herds of giraffes, elephants, and little antelope-like animals strolled across the sunny fields, some stopping at a busy water hole to drink. The lion cub danced joyfully, leaping and prancing around the meadow.

Zuba, Alakay's father, shook a wooden rattle shaped like a lion to get his son's attention. "No, no, Son," Zuba said, laughing. "Over here. See the lion? Get the lion."

Alakay smiled gleefully at the rattle and jumped and rolled on the grass.

His father shook the rattle again. "Now, Son," he said, "if you're going to grow up to be like your daddy someday, you've got to learn how to fight." Zuba tried to sound stern, but he was too happy playing with his new son to be very strict.

Alakay stopped dancing. "Da-da," he mewed, batting at Zuba's nose.

"Okay, Alakay," Zuba said, "let me show you something." He took his son's paw and held it up to his own. The lion and his cub had identical birthmarks on their paws. "We were both born with this mark," Zuba said. "You see, you and I are the same. And when you're bigger, you're going to be Alpha Lion, just like your daddy." He gave his son a tight hug. "Okay, now let's see you fight. Ready?"

The lion cub began to jump and dance again.

Zuba smoothed down his bushy sideburns as he watched his son dance. "No, no, Alakay," the father lion said, but he laughed at his son's antics. "You just amuse yourself, don't you? You're a strange kid." Zuba chuckled and shook the rattle. "Now, c'mon, let's try it again."

Another adult male lion slunk up behind Zuba, raising an eyebrow when he saw Alakay dancing. This lion's name was Makunga, and he had a watchful, sly expression on his face as he sat down beside Zuba. "It's so disappointing when they don't grow up the way you want them to," Makunga remarked.

Zuba scowled at Makunga, obviously not pleased to see him. He turned back toward his dancing son and sighed. "You're not challenging me again, are you?"

A butterfly fluttered by Alakay's head. Alakay yawned once and then started dancing again, imitating the butterfly's wings with his arms.

"Look on the bright side, Zuba," Makunga said. "After I defeat you and take over as Alpha Lion, you'll have so much more time to spend with your kid." Makunga stood up, took a step backward, and crouched in a fighting stance. "We'll fight on three," he declared. "One . . ."

"Pay attention, Alakay," Zuba called to his son, looking away from Makunga. "Watch this. Daddy will show you how it's done—"

"Two, three!" Makunga yelled quickly, and he charged at Zuba.

Before Makunga hit him, Zuba spun around and pummeled his opponent. The two lions grappled on their hind legs, grunting as they heaved against each other in battle. They broke apart and swatted at each other, snarling, their claws extended.

The butterfly flickered past Alakay, capturing the cub's attention. "Fly-fly," he said with a giggle. Alakay clumsily swiped his little paw at the insect and missed. He leaped at it, and missed again. The butterfly zoomed away, and Alakay scampered after it, tumbling into a patch of tall grass.

When Alakay righted himself, he noticed a puffy bit of fur twitching behind him— his tail. He tried to pounce on it and rolled deeper into the weeds, away from the adult lions' battle.

On the other side of the tall grass, Alakay discovered the knotted end of a thick rope. He sprang toward it, but it was yanked just out of his grasp. Alakay jumped at the rope again, and once again it slipped out of reach. He slunk after the sliding rope as it slithered back toward a fence on the far end of the field.

Meanwhile, Zuba had pinned down Makunga on a patch of dry dirt. "Uncle!" Makunga gasped, struggling to breathe under the bigger lion's weight.

"Who's the Alpha Lion?" Zuba demanded.

"You are!" Makunga wheezed.

Zuba breathed heavily in Makunga's face. "And don't you forget it!" he snarled before releasing his defeated challenger. Zuba hopped up and dusted himself off. He turned around to where his son had been. "And that, Alakay, is how you attack—"

But his little cub was nowhere to be seen.

"Alakay?" Zuba called.

On the other side of the field, near the wildlife-reserve border fence, Alakay pounced on the rope knot again, and this time he snagged it in his claws. As he gnawed on the knot, he glanced up. A man in a hunting outfit loomed above him, holding the other end of the rope. "Here, kitty, kitty," the man cooed.

Alakay stumbled back, scared, and bumped into a pair of big boots. A second hunter had snuck up behind him and was now pointing the barrel of a rifle down at the lion cub. "Ah, this one's a beauty," the hunter said. He grabbed Alakay by the scruff of his neck and tossed him into a wooden crate.

The first hunter leaned back on a sign on the fence that read WILDLIFE RESERVE—NO HUNTING OR POACHING. "His fur will be worth a few bucks," he said, pleased.

"It just gets easier and easier," the second

hunter replied. He sealed the crate with a lid and loaded it onto a nearby truck. The poachers climbed into the truck and fired up the engine.

Alakay peered out of the crate's air hole, terrified. "Da-da?" he mewed desperately.

Zuba raced through the tall grass, parting the weeds as he searched for his son. "Alakay?" he hollered. He stood on his hind legs, scanning the savanna to the horizon. "Alakay!"

Then Zuba faintly heard his son calling, "Da-da!"

Zuba whirled around and spotted the truck speeding away. "Oh, no!" Zuba moaned. He took off at top speed toward the truck, bounding through the grass.

"Da-da!" Alakay cried. Through the air hole, he could see his father catching up to the vehicle.

With a mighty leap, Zuba landed in the back of the truck. "Alakay, hold on," he ordered. "Daddy's got you." Zuba clawed at the ropes holding the crate in place, severing them.

The blast of a gunshot knocked Zuba out of the truck.

"Da-da!" Alakay screamed, watching his father tumbling on the ground in a cloud of thick dust.

Near the bank of a river, the truck swerved sharply to avoid a fallen tree trunk, and Alakay's crate broke free.

The crate crashed onto the riverbank and bounced down the steep slope. It plunged into the river, where the rapids swiftly swept it downstream.

Zuba rolled over, and held up his front paw to cover the bullet wound on his bloody ear. He staggered toward the disappearing truck, but he stumbled, teetering on his feet, his vision blurry. There was no way he could catch up.

"Alakay!" he cried out before slumping down onto the dirt.

The river carried the bobbing crate with Alakay inside all the way to the coast of Africa and dumped it in the sea. Alakay huddled miserably inside the crate, whimpering, as the small box floated out into the immensity of the Atlantic Ocean.

The crate caught a swift current and sailed out onto the open ocean, crossing the mighty body of water.

A long time later, the crate finally drifted past the Statue of Liberty, washing ashore on Ellis Island, near New York City. Immigration officials spotted the crate and pulled it onto the island, where they pried it open. They stepped back in surprise when they saw the little lion inside.

Squinting in the sunlight, Alakay peeped up at them with an exhausted, "Mew?"

That day, headlines on all the city newspapers read MYSTERIOUS LION CUB FISHED FROM SEA!

The city officials brought Alakay to the New York Zoo and renamed him Alex. His arrival brought a big crowd eager to see the amazing lion cub who had somehow survived an ocean voyage.

When the zookeepers placed Alex on the big rock in his new pen, Alex was nervous about all the strange people staring into his enclosure. He stood up shakily on his rock. Not knowing what else to do, Alex struck a dramatic dance pose. "Mew?" he murmured uneasily.

The crowd went wild, cheering for the cub. Alex immediately loved the attention and continued to pose for his audience as the people took pictures of the zoo's new star. Alex smiled as he soaked in the applause.

Along the walls of Alex's pen, three animals' heads popped up from their own enclosures, wondering what all the fuss was about. Alex's neighbors were a baby zebra named Marty, a young hippopotamus named Gloria, and a little giraffe named Melman.

"I don't like the looks of this guy," Marty complained.

"Aw," Gloria replied, "I think he's cute."

Marty snorted. "I think he's kind of a show-off."

Melman craned his neck toward Gloria, looking worried. "What?" he asked jealously. "You think he's cute?" Then the baby giraffe started coughing.

Alex kept performing for the cheering crowd. He leaped into the air and spun with his arms outstretched in delight.

Many years later, fireworks exploded above Alex's pen as the crowd went wild, like it had every day for all the years he'd been performing his snazzy act.

Behind him, Marty, Gloria, and Melman, all grown up now, peered over their walls from the same places where they'd watched him for all those years.

"Whoo-hoo," Marty commented flatly. "I still think he's kind of a show-off."

Melman let out a long sigh. "You got to give it to him," he added. "The guy's an animal."

"Maybe he should take a break," Marty said. He tapped his hoof against his mouth. "You know, we could all use a vacation."

Gloria laughed. "Come on," she asked, "where on *earth* would we go on vacation?"

"I don't know about you," Marty replied, "but I want to go to Connecticut."

That night, a special report interrupted TV programming across the city. A newscaster showed wobbly video footage of the zoo animals wandering the streets of New York, and another shot of them on the subway. "On the loose!" the newscaster announced. "Several animals, including the world-famous Alex the lion, 'The King of New York,' escaped from the New York Zoo tonight. The escapees were finally cornered in Grand Central Station."

The news report cut to a video of the inside of Grand Central, where an old woman was kicking Alex in the groin. They showed a close-up of the old woman's face with the words NANA: GRAND CENTRAL HERO identifying her on the bottom of the screen. "He was a very bad kitty!" Nana screeched. When she saw that the camera was focused on her, she yelled, "What are you looking at?" and whacked the camera with her purse.

The reports continued the next night, with footage of crates being loaded onto a ship. "Tragedy on the high seas!" the reporter exclaimed. "The freighter charged with shipping New York's recaptured zoo animals back to their natural home was reported missing today."

And then finally, a night later, the news showed a crowd of New Yorkers holding a candlelight vigil in the New York Zoo. "Tonight hundreds of people have gathered to mourn the tragic disappearance of their beloved zoo animals," the reporter said sadly. "The question on everyone's mind is . . . where are they now?"

It wouldn't be entirely accurate to call the New York Zoo animals' trip to Madagascar a *vacation*, but it certainly had been an exciting adventure.

And today they had finally figured out a way to return home.

At the base of a giant baobab tree, a lemur pulled a bamboo lever with his small paw. The lever set in motion a series of vines passing through big wooden pulleys. The vines hoisted up a bamboo elevator through scaffolding along the outside of the massive tree trunk.

The elevator emerged above the leafy canopy at the edge of a rough, homemade airport perched on the treetop. On one end of the runway, an old, battered airplane waited. The words NEW YORK OR BUST! were scrawled on the airplane's rusty body.

Dozens of little lemurs watched as the elevator's doors opened, revealing Alex, Marty, Gloria, and Melman boogying to funky music. "You've got to move it, move it!" the foursome sang. "You've got to move it—"

*"Move it!"* the lemurs shouted, cheering.

"That song never gets stale," Marty said as he, Gloria, Alex, and Melman stepped into the crowd of excited furry animals. They gave out high-fives and waved to the lemurs as they walked toward the airplane.

"We're going to miss you little fuzz-buckets!" Alex called out. "You guys have been a great crowd!"

"We were glad to introduce you to the toilet," Melman added.

When they reached the top of the stairs leading up to the airplane, Alex turned back toward the crowd of lemurs. "If you ever come to Manhattan, feel free to call first!" he told the little animals. Alex peered down at two lemurs below the stairs. They were picking their noses. Alex grimaced as they swapped boogers . . . and ate them. "Seriously, though," Alex moaned. "Call first."

Before the New Yorkers climbed onto the airplane, a chubby aye-aye named Maurice pushed through the crowd of lemurs. Maurice wheeled an enormous cake to the base of the stairs. BON VOYAGE, PANSIES! was written in frosting on the cake. The lemurs cheered loudly for the treat.

"Settle down, everybody!" Maurice ordered. "Be quiet!" He glared up at Alex, Melman, Marty, and Gloria on top of the stairs. "You can't leave without this!" he announced.

The foursome jumped back a step when the top of the cake suddenly burst open. King

Julien XIII, a ring-tailed lemur, popped up out of the cake. "Hey, surprise, freaks!" Julien yelled in his exotic accent. He was wearing his fancy crown, with a gecko named Stevie perched atop it in his usual place. Julien was also wearing a bikini top made out of coconuts. "Shake it!" he shouted, wiggling his torso. "Look, I'm a lady, everyone! I'm a lady . . . not really. It's me, King Julien!"

Julien laughed. He gazed up at the foursome on the stairs. "Hey, freaks!" he called. "You will be very glad to hear that I am coming with you!"

"Oh," Alex said flatly. "No, thank you."

"Yes, thank you," Julien shot back. "It's my plane." He plucked Stevie off his crown and raised him toward the lemur crowd. "Until I return with the spoils from the new country," he declared, "Stevie will be in charge."

The lemurs fell silent, all of them focusing nervously on the small gecko. Stevie licked his own eye. The lemurs murmured uneasily.

"I don't think they like that idea so much, Julien," Maurice whispered.

Julien held Stevie to his ear. "What is that

you're saying, Stevie? No! That's not even possible, you naughty little thing. He says to let them eat cake!"

The lemurs shouted and jumped around happily.

"Oh!" a squeaky voice called from the crowd. "King Julien, wait for me!" A tiny mouse lemur named Mort rushed out of the elevator, pulling a big suitcase. "I'm all packed. I've brought many hats and snacks!"

Julien cringed. "Oh, no, it's Mort," he hissed at Maurice. "How did he find me?"

"He must have chewed through the ropes," Maurice replied.

Julien clapped his hands together sharply. "Stop that thing!" he ordered the lemurs. "He's carrying scissors and hand cream!"

A group of lemur security guards rushed at Mort and tackled the wee lemur.

"Yeah!" King Julien shouted, shaking a fist. He hopped out of the cake and scrambled up the airplane stairs, where he started to shove the foursome into the plane. "Everyone in! Quickly!" Julien shouted. He had to brace his whole body to push Gloria into the small door. "Get in!"

Inside the plane's decrepit cockpit, the four penguins, Skipper, Kowalski, Rico, and Private, prepared for takeoff.

Skipper pushed a dusty skeleton of the original pilot off its seat and sat down. He peered out the cockpit window at a humongous slingshot set up around the plane. "That's got to be the second biggest slingshot I've ever seen," Skipper said. "But it's going to have to do."

He grabbed the old intercom microphone off the control panel. "Attention!" Skipper announced. "This is your captain speaking! This is going to be a long flight."

Back in the passenger cabin, two chimpanzees named Mason and Phil were already in their seats. The chimps were playing chess on a board spread out on their laps.

Mason reached over and yanked a chess piece out of Phil's mouth. "Phil, stop sucking on the queen," Mason said irritably.

Behind the chimpanzees, Alex, Gloria, Melman, and Marty settled down in their seats as best they could, ignoring the dirt, the cobwebs, and the skeletons of the original passengers.

"New York City, here we come, baby!" Gloria cheered.

The intercom crackled with static. "We'd like you to sit back, relax," Skipper announced, "and pray this hunk of junk flies."

"Um . . . what?" Alex muttered nervously.

Up in the cockpit, Kowalski peered down at the control panel from his co-pilot seat. He flipped a switch and the engines roared to life. "We are a go, sir," Kowalski reported.

Outside the plane, Mort banged on the door with his tiny fists. "I'm outside!" he cried. When the engines fired, Mort was blown clear off the stairs, screaming.

In the passenger cabin, all the animals stared at Private, who was demonstrating the plane's safety procedures. "In case of a loss in cabin pressure," Private mumbled, "place the mask over your face to hide your terrified expression from the other passengers."

Marty tried to fasten his seat belt over his stomach, but the straps were so old that their fasteners disintegrated when he pulled them. He waved to Private. "Excuse me, Miss!" he called, holding up the shredded seat belt. "Aren't these supposed to be attached to my seat?"

"No, sir," Private replied.

In the cockpit, Skipper peered through the windshield. His face tightened with stern determination. "Okay, boys," he ordered. "Launch!"

Rico leaned outside the cockpit's broken side window and pointed at a group of three lemurs behind the plane, who were standing beside thick vines holding the plane's tail to the baobab tree. "Hi!" he growled.

The lemurs all raised their gleaming machetes. "Launch!" they screamed, and they chopped the vines.

With a loud *sproing!* the giant slingshot snapped loose, hurtling the plane into the sky at unbelievable speed.

The force of the takeoff squished everyone in the plane deep into their seats.

The plane wobbled in the air but straightened out again as it passed behind a hill. It soared over the ocean and rose into the clouds as it flew over the Mozambique Channel, which separated the island of Madagascar from the African continent.

Its engines sputtering, the airplane roared into the distance, trailing plumes of black smoke in its wake.

# 2

The plane flew into a purple thunderhead and was swallowed up in a dark storm high above Africa. The clouds flashed with lightning.

Alex was sleeping peacefully in his seat. A jag of lightning sizzled right outside his window, startling him awake. He sat up with a short shriek.

It took a second for Alex to catch his breath, but he calmed down when he realized it was only lightning. He peered out the window at the storm.

Outside in the rain, a small creature scuttled across the airplane wing.

"Ahh!" Alex screamed. "Gremlin!"

Another flash of lightning lit up the wing, and Alex saw that the creature was just Mort, holding on for his life. Alex let out a long breath and relaxed. "Oh, hey, Mort," he said, waving.

"Hi," Mort replied. He waved back, letting go for just a second, and was swept off the wing. Mort screamed as he flew through the air.

Alex cringed, lowered his window blind, and turned away from the window. "That was weird," he muttered to himself.

On the other side of the aisle, Marty leaned over. "Bad dream?" he asked.

Alex shrugged. "I think I just saw Mort on the wing of the plane," he replied.

Melman stuck his head on his long neck up behind Alex. "You've got Madagascar on the brain," he suggested.

"Yeah," Alex said, "it was incredible, wasn't it?"

"I know I'm going to miss it," Gloria added from her seat behind Marty. "It was quite a vacation."

"I think it'll seem much more fun the farther away we get from it," Alex said.

Marty raised an eyebrow. "Like when you bit me on the butt?"

Gloria giggled, fanning her face with her hoof.

Alex blushed. "I'm going to take that thing you're holding on to," he said, forcing himself to sound cheerful, "and I'm going to use it onstage. It's all part of my little actor's bar of emotional tidbits."

Marty chuckled. "Now, are the butts next to the croutons at this salad bar?"

Melman hooted with laughter.

"Marty, don't be sarcastic," Alex replied evenly. "You'll see. The show—POW! Through the roof. It's going to the next level for me when we get home."

All four friends fell quiet for a long moment, thinking about the good old New

York Zoo—*home*. The easy meals delivered right to their enclosures, the crowds of children cheering, the safe familiarity of the city, the expert veterinarians . . .

"Hey, guys," Gloria said, breaking the silence. "I was thinking . . . when we get back, I might just sign up for the breeding program."

Melman's eyes popped open wide. "Breeding program?" he asked.

Gloria nodded. "I think we all reach a point in our lives when we want to meet somebody," she replied. "You know, settle down. Have a relationship?"

"I can see that," Marty said.

Melman peered anxiously at Gloria. "What, you mean—" He coughed nervously. "Like dating?"

"Yeah," Gloria answered. "Dating."

Melman scrunched up his long neck. "Other—other—other . . . ," he stammered, "other guys?"

"What do you mean, other guys?" Gloria demanded.

His lips twitching as he tried to think of a good reply, Melman remained quiet for so long, his eyes bulging, that Alex and Marty started to stare at him. "I'm going to—" Melman began. He shifted in his seat uncomfortably. "What is holding up that beverage service?" he asked. "I'm going to go check." He extended his neck past his friends toward the curtain at the front of the cabin.

Gloria yawned and slid a sleep mask over her eyes. "You guys keep talking," she said. "I'm going to catch a few winks."

Jutting his head past the curtain, Melman found Julien and Maurice sitting in the First Class cabin, watching a movie about crazy airplane crashes. Beside them was another skeleton. Dressed in his stewardess outfit, Private was serving Julien and Maurice champagne and appetizers.

"We just wanted to check on the drinks we ordered," Melman told Private.

"So sorry," Private replied coolly. "Been a little backed up."

Melman glanced down at Julien, who was glaring at the giraffe. "I guess I'll go back to—" Melman began, but he was interrupted by Julien jumping on his snout, pushing him back behind the curtain.

"Come on!" Julien screeched. "Get out! And good-bye!"

"—our section," Melman finished as he exited.

Julien jumped back into his chair. He nudged Maurice with his shoulder. "Whatever happened to the separation of the classes?"

Maurice shrugged. "I'm sure this whole democracy thing is just a fad."

Meanwhile, up in the cockpit, Skipper wasn't paying attention as the fuel gauge needle suddenly dropped down past a red line into "EMPTY." Skipper nuzzled a hula dancer doll on the dashboard with his beak, and giggled as she wobbled against his cheek.

"Skipper, look," Kowalski said, pointing out a small red light flashing on the control panel.

Skipper sat up straight. "Analysis," he ordered.

Kowalski peered at the flashing light. "It looks like a small incandescent bulb, designed to indicate something out of the ordinary," he replied. "Like a malfunction."

Skipper's eyes widened as he stared at the bulb. "I find it pretty and somewhat hypnotic."

"That, too, sir," said Kowalski.

"Right," Skipper said abruptly, snapping out of his trance. "Rico, manual."

Rico rummaged around on his navigator's desk, grabbed a worn book, and tossed it to Skipper.

Skipper caught the manual, raised it up, and smashed the blinking light with it. "Problemo solved."

Kowalski shook his head. "Sir, we may be out of fuel."

"What makes you think that?" Skipper demanded.

"Well," Kowalski answered, "we've lost Engine One." He looked out the window as the propellers on that engine stopped turning. "And Engine Two is no longer on fire."

"Buckle up, boys!" Skipper ordered, pulling his seat belt across his chest.

Skipper grabbed the intercom microphone. "Attention!" he announced. "This is your captain speaking. I've got good news and bad news. The good news is, we'll be landing immediately." He glanced out the window, down at the misty, rocky landscape below. "The bad news is, we're *crash* landing."

The plane echoed with screams as it instantly dropped, diving downward.

"When it comes to air travel," Skipper continued on the intercom, "we know you have no choice whatsoever, but thanks again for choosing Air Penguin!"

Marty, Melman, and Alex hollered in terror as the plane plummeted. Marty and Alex gripped their seats tightly, but Melman tumbled up the aisle, crashing into the luggage rack in the back of the plane. Luggage dropped down onto his head.

"Oh, my gosh!" Melman gasped.

In the First Class cabin, Julien stuck his paws into the air like he was on a rollercoaster. "Raise your arms, Maurice!" he screamed with a crazy laugh. "It's more fun!" Waving his arms around, Julien accidentally opened the emergency door next to him.

The wind ripped the door clean off its hinges.

Julien and Maurice both shrieked and clung to the skeleton. When Julien grabbed on, the parachute on the skeleton deployed, streaming out the open emergency door. It filled with wind and yanked the skeleton, Julien, and Maurice out into the cold air.

"Long live me!" Julien hollered as the parachute carried them up, up, and away.

Inside in the coach cabin, Alex and Marty exchanged fearful looks.

"This could be it, Marty!" Alex shouted over the sound of the rushing wind. "I just want you to know you're truly a one-in-a-million friend."

"Thanks, buddy," Marty said. "You're the best ever."

They shared a smile, but then Alex's grin faded. "I know you won't mind," Alex said, "when I tell you . . ."

"Tell me anything!" Marty called.

Alex squeezed his eyes shut. "I broke your MP3 player," he admitted.

"What?" Marty screeched. "The horror!"

"The buttons were so small," Alex tried to explain. "It made me mad. I'm sorry."

Marty glared at Alex. "I had, like, ten thousand songs on that thing!"

Alex laughed. "Neil Diamond didn't make ten thousand songs."

His face flushed with fury, Marty lunged at Alex and started slapping him. "So now you're dissing Neil Diamond!" he yelled. "I'm going to kill you! Butt-biter!"

Alex raised his paws, protecting his face. "It was an accident," he protested. "I'll get you a new one—"

Suddenly, Melman raised his head in the back of the plane. "I love you, Gloria!" he confessed. "I always have!"

Alex and Marty froze in mid-slap. First

they glanced at Gloria, who was still sleeping soundly, and then they turned to stare at Melman.

Melman pulled back his neck sheepishly. "Like you love the beach," he said quickly. "Or a good book. Or the beach."

At that moment, with the plane still plummeting, Private finally got around to delivering their drinks.

"Okay, Rico, you've had your fun," Skipper said. "Pull up."

Rico yanked hard on his steering wheel, and the plane leveled out in the air, just a few feet above the rocky ground. It cruised over a field of tawny scrub brush.

"Gear down," Skipper ordered. "Gently now. You just want to kiss the ground. Just a little peck . . . a smooch."

Rico deployed the landing gear and lowered the plane. The wheels snagged on the ridge of a dusty hill and sheared off. The plane flopped onto its belly, skidding across the grassy savanna.

"I said kiss it!" Skipper yelled.

Out of control now, the plan careened toward a copse of sturdy trees. Rico steered wildly to avoid collision, but the trees tore off the plane's wings and tail.

"Now a little brake," Skipper added. "Just a touch . . . a little whisper."

Past the trees was a sheer cliff. Everyone aboard screamed as the plane slid off the edge and plummeted toward the ground below.

"Commence emergency landing procedure!" Skipper hollered. "Flaps up! Deploy!"

Rico and Kowalski raised their flippers and pulled emergency parachute straps above them. Giant parachutes popped open above the plane. After an abrupt jolt in the air, the parachutes carried the plane gently down, where it landed lightly in a field of tall grass.

In the coach cabin, Marty and Alex let go of their tight grips on their seats. Oxygen masks popped out of the overhead compartments and dangled in their faces.

An oxygen mask bumping her nose woke up Gloria. She stretched and yawned. "Oh, we're here," she said sleepily. Then she noticed that the cabin was completely in upheaval, with gaping gashes in the walls where the wings had been torn off. Melman sucked desperately on an oxygen mask in the corner. "What in the world?" Gloria asked.

A few seconds later, all four rushed out of a hole in the side of the plane, tumbling onto the ground. They shook off their fear, happy to be on solid ground. Melman was still wearing his oxygen mask.

"I'm okay!" Marty cheered.

"What did you all do to the plane?" Gloria demanded.

"The plane crashed," Marty replied. "I'm alive!"

"See?" Gloria retorted. "I can't even sleep for a minute—" She stopped speaking and took a good look at where she was standing. The flat yellow grasslands around the wrecked plane stretched endlessly into the distance, with strange trees and odd shrubs springing up on the horizon. The bright sunlight beat down, blisteringly hot, while a warm wind rustled the tops of the dry weeds around them.

Gloria put her hands on her hips. "This is *not* the New York airport."

# 3

"**K**owalski, casualty report!" Skipper ordered.

Kowalski shifted a few beads around on his abacus. "Only two passengers unaccounted for, Skipper."

"That's a number I can live with!" Skipper announced. "Good landing, boys! Who says a penguin can't fly?"

The four penguins raised their flippers and gave high fives all around.

Alex approached them. "Hey, happy slappers," he asked, "is there some reason to celebrate?" He gestured toward the airplane, which was a smoking ruin with a crumpled body, no wings, and no tail. "Look at the plane!"

"We'll fix it," Skipper replied confidently. "We'll use grit, spit, and a whole lot of duct tape. We should be up and running in, say . . . six to nine months."

"Sixty-nine months?" Alex gasped.

"No," Skipper said. "Six *to* nine months." He tilted his head toward Kowalski. "I say we use this setback to our advantage," he told the other penguin. "I want you to reconfigure the design . . . so start reconfiguring!"

Alex shook his head, worried. "How did you estimate that amount of time?"

Skipper ignored Alex's question. "You," he told Alex. "Pretty boy. Why don't you and your friends dig a latrine, and maybe find water?"

"Hold on a second," Alex said. "Who made you king of the plane wreck?"

Skipper narrowed his eyes. "Excuse me?" he shot back dangerously. "Fine. You can be in charge. *You* fix the plane."

"Who gives you the authority to put me in charge?" Alex demanded.

Skipper shrugged. "Okay, then, I'll remain in charge."

"Yeah, that's right," Alex declared. "You *will* remain in charge."

"And you and your little hippie friends can stay out of our hair," Skipper added.

"Correctomundo," Alex replied, trying to act tough. "Because *I* decided that."

Skipper crossed his flippers. "Good for you."

"Yeah, well . . ." Alex continued, running out of steam. "Guess what? This discussion isn't over!" With that, he stomped away.

Skipper called over to Mason and Phil, who had continued to play chess during the whole crash and were still playing it now. "Higher mammals!" Skipper shouted to the chimpanzees. "You stay with us. We can use your front cortexes and opposable thumbs."

Calmly, Phil flashed a series of sign language hand signals at the penguin.

"Phil!" Mason gasped. "I should wash your hands out with soap!"

Gloria caught up with Alex as he stormed away from the plane. "How are they going to fix this plane?"

Alex stopped and rubbed his paws through his mane. "You know," he said weakly, "a lot of grit and spit and . . . stick-to-itiveness."

Marty shuddered. "That doesn't sound too promising."

Alex started pacing in circles in the field. "You're right!" he cried. "We're stuck here!"

Marty raced in front of Alex, trying to calm him. "Hey," he said, "as long as we're together, we'll be okay."

Alex covered his face with his paws. "Yeah, we're together. It's a love fest. But love ain't going to get us home, guys."

Right then, a truck appeared over a small hill and stopped behind Alex. It was filled with tourists, and a sign on the door read AFRICAN SAFARIS. The tour guide stood up in the driver's seat. "Behold!" he announced. "The lion!"

Alex whirled around and gaped at the truck. "Hey, it's people!" he said. Alex blinked as all the tourists took his picture, dazzling him with flashes.

The tour guide slid back down in his seat. "Okay, there is much to see," he said. "Moving on." The truck started up again across the grassland.

It took a second for the New Yorkers' shock to wear off, but when it did, they raced after the truck.

"Wait!" Alex yelled.

"People!" Melman bleated. "It's people!"

"They'll help us!" Gloria added.

"Stop!" Marty cried.

Desperate for a ride back to civilization, Alex ran the fastest, passing his friends. He began to catch up to the truck. The tourists all turned around and took his picture.

"Wait!" Alex screamed. "If you stop, I'll autograph those!"

To the tourists, Alex's words just sounded like roaring. It slowly dawned on them that this wasn't just a great photo opportunity—they were being chased.

"The lion's gaining on us!" one man shouted. "Step on it!"

"He's attacking!" a woman shrieked.

Alex peered up into the truck just as one elderly woman lowered her camera. Her eyes widened as she recognized him . . . and Alex recognized her, too. It was Nana, the old lady who beat him senseless with her purse in Grand Central Station. "I know you," Nana said, her lips pressing in a tight line.

"You." Alex gasped.

"It's the bad kitty!" Nana scolded. She whapped him with her purse again.

"Ow!" Alex complained. "Give me that!" He snatched her bag, stealing it from her.

Alex's yank pulled her right out of the truck. She rolled and came up in a fighting stance as the truck screeched to a halt behind her.

With a scary yell, Nana launched herself at

Alex. She and the lion traded punches. Alex knocked out her dentures, which flew into the weeds.

"How do you like that?" Alex taunted.

In reply, Nana knocked out one of Alex's real teeth. Then she leaped in the air and kicked him three times. *"Uno, dos, tres!"* she hollered. When Nana landed, she hoisted up a huge log, ready to bash Alex with it.

Alex grabbed the log and tossed it aside. Then he picked up a big rock and threatened to clobber Nana.

Nana kicked him in the groin. Alex slowly fell to one side, out for the count.

"Ooh," Marty said, wincing in sympathy. "Right in the batteries."

Nana patted her hair, picked up her teeth, and popped them back in her mouth. "Think an old lady can't take care of herself?" she huffed.

As she stomped back toward the truck, all the tourists applauded wildly. The tour guide opened the door for her.

"Thank you, dear," Nana said kindly.

Marty and Gloria rushed over to help Alex to his feet. "Are you out of your mind?" Gloria asked. "We need their help and you're harassing little old ladies?"

Alex smiled and held up Nana's purse. He rummaged around in it and pulled out a cell phone. "Aha!" he cried triumphantly. "Who's out of my mind now?"

"Guys!" Melman called from the top of a hill nearby.

Ignoring Melman, Alex started dialing a number on the phone.

"See if you can get an operator," Marty told Alex.

"No problem," Alex said, holding the phone up to his ear. "Out of my mind . . . we're going home!" Listening on the phone, he absentmindedly followed Marty and Gloria as they trudged up the hill. Melman was gesturing frantically for them all to hurry.

When they reached the top, Marty's and Gloria's jaws dropped when they saw the view on the other side.

Alex pressed buttons on the cell phone,

swearing under his breath. "I think we're out of range," he said. "I can't even get a signal."

"Look," Marty told him.

"What?" Alex asked, glaring at the phone.

Marty lowered the phone with his hoof and directed Alex's gaze to the scene spread out before them.

"Oh," Alex said. "Wow."

Far in the horizon a mountain poked up into the clouds, with the sun blazing on its snowy, smoking peak. In the middle distance, herds of giraffes, elephants, and other animals strolled across the flat, sunny fields. About a mile away was a busy water hole, crowded with lions, zebras, hippopotami, and rhinoceros lazing around, socializing, drinking the cool water in the oasis, or bathing in the sparkling pool.

"All those zebras, like me," Marty said. "Where are we?"

"San Diego," Melman replied. "This time I'm forty percent sure."

"I know this place," Alex said, his voice sounding far away.

"I think it's Africa," Marty breathed. "It's got to be. Our ancestral crib. It's in our blood. I can feel it."

"No, no," Alex said. "It's like déjà vu . . . like . . . like I've been here before."

The four friends rushed down into the valley below, racing toward the water hole. As they got closer, they slowed down, getting nervous about approaching the wild animals.

When they were in speaking distance, Alex called out, "How!"

All the animals at the water hole turned to look.

"How," Alex repeated awkwardly. "Me Alex. Me and my friends fly. Fly in great metal bird."

Two nearby lions glanced at each other, confused.

"Then plummet!" Alex continued, dancing out the motions of his story. "Smash ground. Go boom! Then here we emerge. We offer only happiness and good greetings."

"Is he dancing about a *plane crash*?" one hippo asked another in disbelief.

"Uh . . . yeah," Alex replied. "I thought . . . sorry."

"You mean you came from off the reserve?" a giraffe piped up.

"Yeah," Alex answered. "Way off. From the New York Zoo, actually."

The crowd of animals around the water hole murmured in amazement and gathered closer. But then a loud roar came from behind the animals, and they parted to let a mature lion and his mate through.

The big lion roared again . . . but broke off, coughing. His mate patted his back. "Don't strain yourself," she said.

"What's all this hubbub?" the big lion demanded.

An elephant stepped forward and bowed his head to the lion. "They say they're from . . . *off the reserve*."

"That's impossible," the lion retorted. "Only people come from off the reserve." He strode over to the strangers and glared at them.

"You look familiar," Alex told the lion. "Do I know you from—?"

"How could you possibly survive the hunters?" the lion interrupted.

"We didn't see any hunters," Gloria replied.

Alex couldn't stop staring at the big lion. There was just something so familiar about him . . .

"What are you looking at?" the lion roared at Alex.

"Me?" Alex squeaked. "Nothing."

The lion strode very close to Alex, getting in his face. "This water hole doesn't need any more mouths to feed. So skedaddle back to wherever you came from!"

Alex took a step backward. "Okay, well, is there maybe, like, a manager we could talk to?"

The lion narrowed his eyes. "Oh, I see," he said. "You're here to challenge me."

"What?" Alex replied, raising his paws. "No, no challenge—"

Puffing himself to his full height, the lion

loomed over Alex. "Well, that's what it looks like to me!"

The lion's mate darted between him and Alex. "Wait, Zuba," she said.

"Doggone, Florrie," Zuba complained. "Don't you see I'm trying to take care of business here?"

"Yeah, yeah, Zuba," the lioness replied. "Hold on." She stepped forward, studying Alex's face intently. An expression of amazed surprise widened her eyes. "Alakay . . . ?" she breathed. "Is that you?"

"No, no," Alex said quickly. "It's Alex. *Ix*. Like New York Knicks."

Then Florrie noticed a birthmark on Alex's paw. "Look, Zuba," she said, pointing at the mark.

As soon as Zuba saw the birthmark, he slumped, dropping his aggressive pose.

Alex peered down at his paw. "Oh, I've always had that," he said. "The vet checked it out. It's kind of a beauty spot, really."

Zuba couldn't take his eyes off Alex's paw. "The mark," he whispered.

"All right," Alex said. "This is a little weird now."

"Honey," Zuba said softly, looking up at Alex's face, "he's come home." He raised his own paw, which had a birthmark on it that exactly matched Alex's. The big lion's eyes filled with tears. "You've come home."

"Whoa," Alex breathed, staring at the identical birthmarks.

"Son," Zuba breathed.

Alex gazed at Zuba's face. Now he could see there was a very strong resemblance between himself and the lion. "Dad?" he whispered. He glanced at Florrie, turning his head quickly between the two lions who were beaming at him. "Mom and Dad?"

Zuba and Florrie smiled wider, and then they both nodded.

# 4

"**M**om and Dad," Alex said. A huge smile brightened his face. "It's my mom and dad!" he cheered, tears streaming down his face. He hurled himself into their arms, hugging them happily.

Alex glanced back at Marty, Gloria, and Melman. "I've got a mom and dad!" he told them, overjoyed.

Tears welled up in their eyes, too, as they watched the happy reunion. Marty jumped in and gave Alex's parents a hug.

"My baby is alive!" Alex's mother wailed.

"My son is home!" Zuba roared. He lifted Alex onto his broad shoulders and strode around with his son as the crowd of wild animals erupted in applause.

On the other side of the water hole, Julien and Maurice broke into the crowd, riding bright pink flamingos. "Giddy up, feathered horse!" Julien cried.

"Move it out of the way," Maurice ordered a group of zebras in front of them.

Julien waved to the crowd from atop his flamingo. "Hello, everybody!" he called. "Your new king is here!"

When Zuba shouted, "This calls for a celebration!" on the far side of the crowd, Julien thought the animals' cheering reaction was for him.

"Maurice," Julien told the aye-aye, "I think they like me."

Soon the celebration turned into a full-on

pool party around the water hole. A group of animals bashed out fun, rhythmic music, and everyone started dancing. Julien jumped in front of the dancers and led the disco moves. "I shall call my new kingdom 'Madagafrica!'" he announced.

"Whoo-haa!" the animals yelled as they all stepped in unison, bowing at the same time. "Madagafrica!"

"Madagafri-what?" Julien called out.

"Madagafrica!" the animals replied, shimmying together.

Julien slid over to a band of elephants. "The fat guys, what?"

"Madagafrica!" the elephants trumpeted as they boogied.

"Nice moves!" Julien told them.

Marty wandered through the festivities. "Hey, I'm Marty," he tried to introduce himself to a hippo. The hippo didn't stop his jazz moves. "I'm kind of new around here."

Hearing Marty's voice, a herd of zebras all turned to face him. Marty was shocked that they all looked exactly like him, but then he grinned. "Hey, you're a good-looking group!" he said. "You like to run?"

"Oh, yeah!" one zebra replied, sounding just like Marty, too. "Running is crack-a-lackin!"

"That's right!" Marty said approvingly. "Crack-a-lackin! You guys are speaking my language!"

Melman jumped around to the music in the company of several other giraffes. They all danced awkwardly like giant pogo sticks. During a break in the music, Melman slumped against a tree, catching his breath beside another giraffe named Stephen.

"You really don't have doctors here?" Melman asked.

Stephen shook his head ruefully. "Well, not anymore."

"What if you catch a cold?" Melman wondered.

Another giraffe craned his neck over. "We go over to the dying holes and . . . we die," he replied. He pointed to a place out on the open savanna, where big pits had been dug in the ground. In the pits, Melman could make out the heads of a few sickly giraffes sticking out of the holes, waiting to expire. One of them coughed wretchedly.

"Okay," Melman said, "you guys really need a doctor."

Stephen raised his eyebrows. "Well, we do have an opening."

"Would you be interested?" the other giraffe offered.

A look of pure delight lit up Melman's face. "Me?" he gushed. "A doctor?"

In the middle of the water hole, Gloria wallowed in the deep water among a group of other female hippopotami. They all giggled and splashed around when a bunch of male hippos cannonballed into the water near them, showing off.

"It's raining men!" Gloria said with a laugh. "Hallelujah!" She smiled at the other female hippos. "You all got it going on!"

A sassy female hippo bumped Gloria with

her butt. "Now how come you don't have a man in your life?" she asked. "You got worms?"

"Oh, I've gotten rid of those," Gloria replied. "Listen, girls . . . Manhattan is short on two things: parking and hippos!"

Meanwhile, all the lions had gathered together by a rocky outcropping on the outskirts of the water hole. Alex stood with his parents, surrounded by the entire pride of lions.

"Hey, everyone," Zuba announced. "I just found out my son here is a doggone *king*! He's the King of New York!"

The lions panted in approval, impressed.

Zuba nudged Alex. "Show me some of your moves, Son!"

Alex hopped onto a rock, happy to show off. "This one always knocks them dead!" he announced. Then he let loose his loudest roar, and jumped into his fiercest pose, with the setting sun making his mane glow.

The lions around him applauded.

"Ooh, look out!" Zuba shouted. He leaped onto the rock and threw his arm around his son. "Stick around, and you'll have my job in no time," Zuba said. "I won't be Alpha Lion forever."

All the lions laughed . . . except for one. He was Makunga, Zuba's old enemy.

Nearby, a herd of zebras thundered by, with Marty galloping in the middle of the pack. He grinned as he ran with his fellow zebras, loving their speed and the freedom of the open field. He couldn't get over how similar all the zebras were to him; it was like finding a band of long-lost brothers.

"Welcome to the herd!" one zebra told Marty as they all banked around a bushy tree.

"Me?" Marty gushed. "I'm in the herd? I've always wanted to be part of a herd."

Another zebra zoomed by him. "Here it's one for all . . ."

"And all for all!" a zebra finished. "Y'all!"

Over by the giraffes, Melman was being inducted as their new doctor. He'd been dressed up in an elaborate feathered headdress, and dozens of glittering necklaces had been looped around his neck.

Melman shook his neck so that all the necklaces clinked and clattered. "How do I look?"

Stephen tapped his lips thoughtfully. "Technically, a traditional Witch Doctor has a bone through his nose." He whipped out a big, pointy bone.

Melman stepped backward, covering his nose.

"Don't worry," another giraffe explained. "It's a clip-on."

Melman relaxed and allowed Stephen to clip the bone onto his nose.

"Voilà!" Stephen exclaimed. "He's a Witch Doctor!"

All the giraffes applauded.

"Oh, my mother will be so happy!" Melman gushed.

At the same time, Gloria and the other female hippos stepped out of the water and joined the dancers. They swayed to the music, swinging their ample hips.

Gloria's sassy friend smirked and gestured back toward the water hole, where a pair of almost-submerged eyes was watching Gloria intently. "Don't look now," Gloria's friend said, "but I think Moto Moto likes you."

"Look out!" another girl hippo added. "Here he comes."

Gloria tried to act cool as the biggest hippopotamus she'd ever seen stepped out of the water, droplets glistening on his enormous, muscular body.

The female hippos giggled as Moto Moto took his time swaggering toward them. He pushed a big boulder out of his way like it weighed nothing, and he didn't even notice when he trampled a dik-dik.

When Moto Moto got close, the other hippos made room for him beside Gloria. Moto Moto flexed all his giant muscles, and the female hippos gasped, impressed. Gloria started dancing again, swaying next to Moto Moto.

"Goodness, girl," Moto Moto said suavely, "you huge."

Gloria pursed her lips at him. "Who's your friend?" she asked. "Or is that your butt?"

Moto Moto chuckled in his deep voice. "Girl," he said approvingly, "you're as quick as you are hefty."

Gloria smiled at the compliment. "So . . ." she said, "you're Moto Moto."

"The name so nice," Moto Moto replied, "you say it twice."

"I like it," Gloria said, bumping him with her butt. "Fatso."

Moto Moto winked at her. "I'll see you around, girl," he grunted. "It won't be hard . . . because you so plumpy." He sashayed through the crowd, seductively dancing, knowing she was watching.

Gloria grinned at the big hippo's cool style.

Alex and Zuba were crowd-surfing atop the other lions. When Alex was passed to Makunga, he dropped him. "Oops."

"Um . . ." Makunga began, "I hate to be a party pooper, but uh . . . some of the other lions were wondering when you were going to banish your son."

**ALEX, MARTY, GLORIA, AND MELMAN BID A FOND FAREWELL TO MADAGASCAR.**

**SURPRISE! KING JULIEN AND MAURICE WANT TO GO WITH THE "FREAKS" TO NEW YORK.**

MORT WANTS TO GO, TOO. HE PACKED MANY SNACKS AND HATS.

"SIT BACK, RELAX, AND PRAY THIS HUNK OF JUNK FLIES," SAYS SKIPPER.

**MASON AND PHIL GO BANANAS FOR CHESS.**

**GLORIA GETS SOME BEAUTY SLEEP.**

"THE GOOD NEWS IS, WE'LL BE LANDING IMMEDIATELY."

"THE BAD NEWS IS, WE'RE CRASH-LANDING."

**THEY MADE IT BACK TO THE EARTH!**

**BUT GLORIA WANTS TO KNOW *WHERE* ON EARTH . . .**

THIS ISN'T THE NEW YORK CITY AIRPORT!

"HEY, HAPPY SLAPPERS!" SAYS ALEX. "LOOK AT THE PLANE!"

**"IT'S THE BAD KITTY."**

Zuba lowered himself to the ground and stared at Makunga coldly. "What are you talking about?"

Makunga narrowed his eyes. "They're griping about how Alakay never passed the Rite of Passage. So, technically speaking, he can't be a member of the pride."

"What is this Rite of Passage?" Alex asked.

"It's a tradition," Zuba explained. "Where young lions earn their manes by demonstrating their prowess."

Alex hopped excitedly. "Like a performance? Sort of a show of skill . . . a talent show type of deal?"

Zuba nodded. "Yeah."

"I want to do it!" Alex insisted. "If it's traditional lion stuff, I want to do it. Earn my mane! Show my prowess! I want to *be* Alakai."

"Alakay," his mother corrected him.

"Alakay," Alex amended. "Even better."

Zuba clapped Alex on the back. "That's my boy!" he cheered. Then Zuba turned to face the pack of lions around him. "We need to hold a Rite of Passage first thing in the morning!"

Behind Zuba, a sneaky smile twitched on Makunga's lips.

Later that evening, as the party wound down, the New Yorkers gathered together on top of a big, flat rock to watch the gorgeous African sunset.

Julien wandered over to them, weaving from too much partying. He stumbled, and fell asleep on Gloria's stout leg.

Gloria flicked him off her with her finger.

"Guys . . ." Alex began, leaning back against a gnarled tree trunk with his paws behind his head, "This is where we belong."

Meanwhile, the penguins, wearing leaf camouflage, hid in the tall grass. Rico looked out through the flora with a bottle telescope. The tourist truck rumbled up the road.

"Operation 'Tourist Trap' is a go," Skipper confirmed.

"Oh, I like that one," Private approved.

"It works on many levels, sir," said Kowalski.

"You guys are a bunch of suck-ups," complained Skipper.

"That too, sir," agreed Kowalski.

"Absolutely," nodded Private.

The penguins got into position as the truck got closer.

"Stations! Stage one, go!" ordered Skipper.

Private ran out and fell into the middle of the road as if he'd been hit. The truck screeched to a halt.

"C'mon, take the bait!" chanted Skipper.

The tourists exited the truck, and started taking pictures.

"Oh, no!" cried one man.

"Is he dead?" asked another.

"Ah, look at the poor little guy. Isn't he cute!" whimpered a woman.

"Stage two! Go! Go! Go!" ordered Skipper.

The three other penguins ran to the truck. Skipper flipped Kowalski into the cab while Rico popped the truck's hood as the concerned tourists continued to crowd around Private. Just as Rico hot-wired the engine, Private flew out from under the crowd and into the truck.

"Reverse! . . . Gas!" ordered Skipper.

They floored it, stranding the tourists . . . and Nana.

**5**

That night, all the animals settled down to sleep, exhausted from their day of wild partying. Near the rocky outcropping, the lions tucked in their young cubs and curled around them, keeping them warm through the night.

Zuba led Alex toward the only cave in the outcropping—the home of the

Alpha Lion. Florrie took Alex's arm, patting it fondly, as they entered the cave, which was lit by fireflies and had a cozy, homey feel.

"Are you ready?" Zuba asked, pulling Alex toward the back of the cave, where a flat rock had been set up as a bed. "This is where you always slept."

Alex stared at the small space, flooded by memories. "Oh, man," he whispered. "Wow." He toyed with a wooden mobile that dangled above the bed. "Was this mine?"

As Alex played with his old toy, Zuba stepped back and gazed at his son, glowing with happiness. "Look at you," Zuba said softly. "Look at him, honey!"

Florrie put her head on Zuba's shoulder as they both watched Alex checking out his old room.

"Oh, my," Alex said, picking up a rattle shaped like a lion. "This thing!" He gave it a shake. "I remember this!" He hopped up on his rock bed and bounced on it. "A little harder than I remember—" He leaned back on the bed and spotted a small paw print on the wall. He held up his paw to the print, comparing them. "Is that . . . mine?"

His mother nodded. "You had the cutest paws."

"Little itty bitty ol' paws," Zuba added.

Florrie touched the paw print gently. "You did that the day we lost you."

Alex sat up on the bed. "Wow," he said, glancing at the little paw print. "I was so young . . . what happened to me?"

Zuba ducked his head sadly. "It was all my fault," he said, his voice choking with guilt. "I turned my back for a minute, and . . ." Zuba trailed off, unable to tell his son about that terrible day.

Florrie put her hand on his arm, soothing him as he sat down next to Alex on the bed. "It was not your fault," she told Zuba firmly. Alex's mother gazed into her son's eyes. "Your father did everything he could," she explained. "He tracked those hunters for weeks, searching for you far off the reserve."

"Finally," Zuba added sadly, "I had to

assume that the hunters . . . well . . ."

"We thought they'd killed you," Florrie finished.

Zuba shook off the unpleasant memories and smiled at Florrie. "But my son fought those hunters off, huh?" He threw an arm around Alex proudly. Don't mess with the King of New York!"

"That's right!" Alex crowed, slicing his hand in the air like a karate chop. *"Hi-yaa!"*

Zuba laughed and playfully shoved his son. They traded fake punches. "Keep your chin in!" Zuba advised, chuckling. "Yeah!"

"All right," Florrie said, breaking up the play fight. "You boys better be careful. Watch out before you break something."

When the males had settled down, Alex's mother pulled out a worn blanket woven from soft reeds. "You used to call this Foofie," she told her son.

"Foofie?" Alex asked. He sniffed the blanket, and the smell brought him right back to his childhood. His eyes widened in delight. "Foofie!"

"Woman," Zuba told his mate, "he doesn't want that thing—"

Zuba reached for the blanket, but Alex hugged it to his chest. "Foofie!" Alex cried, sounding like a baby.

Both Zuba and Florrie thought Alex's reaction was a bit strange, and Alex loosened his grip on the blanket and let Zuba take it.

"Zuba, you better give him his Foofie," Alex's mother said.

"No," Alex said quickly. "Thank you. It's perfect." He snatched Foofie back from Zuba and laid it gently beside him on the bed.

Zuba stood up and clapped his hands. "Well, Son," he said, "you get your rest. You've got a big day tomorrow and you're going to need all your strength."

"I'm going to bring the house down for you, Dad," Alex promised.

"I hope so," said Florrie playfully. "Otherwise your father will have to banish you."

Zuba gently chucked Alex under the chin with his fist. "I know you're going to do us proud," he said. "You know why?" He lifted Alex's paw and compared their identical birthmarks again. "You were born with it, Son. Good night, Alakay."

For a long moment, Zuba stood at the foot of the bed, beaming down at Alex, almost unable to believe that his long-lost son was truly returned to him. "My boy," Zuba mumbled. "My own boy . . ." He trailed off as he backed away from the bed, and then turned to leave Alex's area. "My son's a king," he told himself proudly.

Florrie kissed her grown cub on the forehead.

"Good night, Mom," Alex said softly.

"Good night, Alakay," his mother replied. Then she squished a firefly on the wall, turning off the light, before she followed her mate.

As soon as they were gone, Alex scooped up Foofie and nuzzled it with his cheek. "Foofie," he sighed. "Oh, Foofie! My Foofie!"

✿ ✿ ✿

The next day, Alex prepared for the Rite of Passage ceremony with a few young lion cubs. They gathered in a backstage tent behind the arena where the Rite would be held. Alex and the young lions solemnly applied ceremonial body paint on their fur. The cubs painted themselves with traditional African symbols, but Alex painted his whole face white, and added black lipstick and black stars around his eyes like a mime.

"So, little cub scouts," Alex advised, "just remember, a great performance comes from the heart, okay?"

The lion cubs snickered. "Sure, Mister," one cub agreed mockingly.

Makunga sauntered into the tent and slunk up to Alex. "Hey, Alakay," Makunga said, "I thought I'd wish you luck. You're not nervous, are you?"

"Naw," Alex replied. "It's my thing. You know, it's kind of what I do."

Makunga slid his arm around Alex's shoulders and steered him away from the cubs. "In my opinion," Makunga whispered, "the key to this whole thing is choosing the right competitor."

"Competitor?" Alex asked, stopping short. "You mean this is a dance battle . . . a dance-off?"

"Uh," Makunga replied, bewildered, "sure."

"Great!" Alex cheered. "I love that. Freestyle, put your moves out. Who do you think would be a good match for me? You know, just to keep things interesting."

Makunga glanced around, making sure nobody was listening. "I wish I could help," he answered, "but that's strictly against our ancient traditions and all that we hold sacred, but . . . if it was me out there, I'd choose Teetsi."

"Teetsi," Alex repeated. He smiled at Makunga. "Sounds interesting. Thank you."

"Anything for Zuba's boy," Makunga replied.

A loud gong sounded outside.

"Go get 'em, tiger," Makunga said, giving

Alex a shove toward the other cubs, who were lining up at the tent exit.

Alex was last in line. While he was waiting to enter the arena, he shook himself, relaxing his arms and legs, and he did some vocal exercises. "Five, six, seven, eight," he enunciated. "Let's do this."

When the line of lions started jogging forward, Alex followed along into the arena.

A crowd of lions was seated around a big ring of stones. Other lions banged on drums as the cubs entered, and the crowd burst into cheers and applause.

Zuba stood up beside the ring, where a podium was set up. "Let us begin the Rite of Passage ceremony," he announced, holding up his Alpha Lion scepter.

"C'mon, baby!" Florrie shouted beside Zuba. "Make Mama proud!"

"I'm on it, Mom!" Alex shouted back. He took his place in front of the podium with the lion cubs.

"So who will be the first participant?" Zuba asked.

Alex shot his hand up. "Me!"

Zuba glanced at Alex. "Hmm, how about you?" he asked with a wink. "The tall, handsome lion there . . . choose your opponent."

Alex scratched his chin. "Let me see," he said thoughtfully. "I guess I'll pick . . . Teetsi!"

The crowd erupted in surprised gasps.

"Teetsi?" Alex's mother cried. "Why did he pick *Teetsi*?"

"Oh, that's my boy," Zuba told her. "He's got gumption!" He pointed toward the far side of the ring, where the massive, muscular lion Teetsi was snoozing on the ground. "Somebody wake him up," Zuba ordered.

A lion picked up a big boulder and smashed it down on Teetsi's head.

Teetsi sprang up on all fours, growling and snarling. Then he stood up to his full, enormous height, and stomped into the ring. Every step he took flexed a ridiculous amount of muscles in his buff body. Teetsi let out a deafening roar right at Alex in the center of the ring, and the giant lion glared at his challenger with crazy, scary eyes.

Alex started to circle Teetsi, dropping down in a phony battle crouch. "All right," Alex said, taunting his opponent, "so let's do this, Teetsi. Come on, Teetsi fly. Come on, bring it!"

"Let's dance!" Teetsi growled.

"Okay," Alex agreed. He began tap dancing around Teetsi.

Teetsi grimaced in confusion. "Not *dance* dance," he snarled. "Fight!"

"Oh, *dance fight*!" Alex sang. "You got it!" He snapped his fingers and shuffled with fake menace like he was in a Broadway musical.

Bewildered, Teetsi glanced around the arena. All the other lions had the same stunned look on their faces—except for Makunga, who was grinning.

"Is he dancing?" Florrie whispered to Zuba. "I know that boy is not dancing."

"This is going even better than I thought," Makunga muttered to himself, savoring the deliciously embarrassing moment as Alex turned his back to Teetsi and wiggled his hips.

Zuba jumped to his feet. "Alakay!" he hollered. "Turn around!"

"No, no, Pop," Alex called back. "The steps go hop-shuffle-hip-swish, *then* turn around." He spun into his final pose, his arms outstretched with jazz hands.

Then Alex saw Teetsi barreling at him like a runaway freight train.

*Slam!*

The giant lion hit Alex so hard that a huge rift in the ground unzipped across the savanna. Teetsi pummeled Alex into a big boulder, squashing him flat against the rock.

Alex crumpled to the ground, barely conscious. The boulder crumbled to dust.

Zuba and Florrie rushed to Alex's side.

"Oh," Zuba said softly, horrified. "No."

"Alakay . . ." Alex's mother whispered.

"What happened?" Zuba asked. "You said you were a king!"

"It's a stage name," Alex replied, "for when I perform for the people."

The entire crowd of lions remained silent in shock.

Everyone turned to look at Makunga. He strode forward toward the podium and stood next to Zuba, opening his arms wide and facing the crowd. "Who would've ever imagined that today Zuba would have to banish his own son?"

The audience groaned, surprised and upset.

Zuba bit his lip worriedly as he tried to decide what to do. He took his position as Alpha Lion seriously . . . but how could he cast out his only son, who had just been returned to him?

All the lions waited silently for Zuba's decision.

Finally, Zuba lowered his head. "Then I'm not your Alpha Lion anymore," he announced. He threw his scepter on the ground and stepped away from it.

Alex sat up. "Dad, no," he said. "You can't do this."

"No!" Makunga added, pretending to be

horrified. "Who will lead us?" He reached out and grabbed the scepter. He held it out to the crowd of lions. "Who could possibly take Zuba's place? Anyone? Someone must make the sacrifice and assume the role of Alpha Lion."

In the front row, a male lion started to rise.

"You, sir?" Makunga asked. He quickly swung the scepter and bopped the lion on the head, knocking him out cold. "I guess not."

Nobody else rose to take the scepter. Makunga acted humble as he clutched the scepter to his chest. "No one?" he asked. "Well . . . I suppose I could carry this tremendous burden." He waved to Teetsi. "Get the hat," he ordered.

Teetsi rushed out of the arena.

Makunga pointed the scepter at Alex. "As your new leader, it is with a heavy heart and deepest regret that I order Alakay to leave the water hole. He shall wear this Hat of Shame—"

Teetsi ran back over and slammed a tall

hat onto Alex's head. It was a goofy hat, covered with bananas, apples, grapes, and pineapples.

"And Alakay shall live in disgrace," Makunga continued, "for a thousand years . . . or life. Whichever comes last."

The crowd groaned in disappointment.

# 6

In the dry, desolate land of the dik-diks, on the other side of the valley from the water hole, Zuba sat on a hollow log, staring blankly at a scrubby bush ahead of him.

Alex, still wearing his fruit hat, put his arm around his mother. "I was the one who was cast out," he told her. "Why are you guys moving out here?"

Florrie forced herself to smile. "We're a family," she said, "and we've got to stick together."

Zuba exploded. "You should have told us, son," he said, sounding frustrated. "You should have told us that you weren't a real king!"

"Well," Alex said, "You never told me I'd have to fight anybody! I've never fought another lion in my life."

Zuba looked at Alex, confused. "No, I guess not," he sneered. "You perform."

"The point is," Alex continued, "Makunga set me up back there. None of this would have happened . . ."

"If you were a real lion," Zuba interrupted.

Zuba's words hit Alex hard—and broke his heart.

After giving Alex a pat on the knee, Zuba stood. "Come on," he said. "Let's go give your mother a hand." He walked toward their new scrubby bush.

✿ ✿ ✿

Meanwhile, Marty was entertaining hundreds of other zebras at the water hole, performing his trademark water show, which had been a big hit at the New York Zoo. In the big *finale*, Marty spat three spouts of water in the air and caught them one by one, before spitting all the water in his mouth at the crowd.

"Ta-daaaaa!" Marty exclaimed when he was done.

The other zebras cheered his performance. "Nice one, Marty!"

"Bet you haven't seen that before," Marty replied.

"Hey!" a zebra shouted. "Let's all give it a try!"

Marty shrugged. "It's going to take years of practice. You don't just learn something like this overnight. And you're never going to get a tight stream until you build up your lip muscles to the point where you can purse your lips like this." He puckered his lips tightly. "Got it?"

The zebras all filled their mouths with water and then rushed into a perfectly spaced formation on the side of the water hole. Marty watched dumbfounded as hundreds of zebras all spit water into the air together, exactly repeating his performance, and nailing the finale. At the end, they all spouted water at Marty, drenching him. "Ta-daaaaa!" the zebras called in unison.

Marty forced himself to grin at them. He was dripping wet, but that wasn't what bothered him about the show. "How did you do that?" he demanded. "You guys got that right out of the box."

"If you can do it," a zebra answered, "we can do it."

"It's in our blood," another zebra added.

"Oh," Marty said, his grin fading. "I always thought I was a little bit unique."

"We are unique!" all the zebras shouted together.

"We're like a force of nature," one zebra said. "A million points of light—"

"And dark stripes," another zebra broke in.

"Exactly the same!" all the zebras cried.

Marty let out a long, depressed sigh. "Exactly the same," he repeated.

On the other side of the water hole, many of the giraffes had gathered around Melman to watch his first surgery as the giraffe Witch Doctor.

Melman tied off a tight vine as the other giraffes gaped in awe over his shoulder.

"Saw," Melman requested, and a giraffe handed him a short, wooden cutting tool.

He sawed away at something for a moment before saying, "Suture."

Another giraffe passed him a needle and thread, and Melman concentrated on sewing up his patient's injury.

"Swab," Melman ordered. Three giraffes reached over and all dabbed at his sweaty forehead with leaves. Then Stephen leaned over, too close, to watch what Melman was doing.

"You're in my light, Stephen," Melman said.

As Stephen backed up, he noticed something worrisome on Melman's body. "Ooh," he breathed, "you've got a brown spot there on your shoulder."

"Yes," Melman replied calmly. "That's very observant of you, Stephen. As you can see, I'm covered in brown spots." He tied another vine into place and raised his neck. "Okay. That bone will be good as new in a few weeks."

Melman's patient, a young giraffe, sat up on the operating rock. He peered down at the splint on his leg. It looked very professionally done. "So," the young giraffe asked nervously, "I don't have to pick out a dying hole?"

"No, Timo," Melman answered. "You've got your whole life ahead of you."

Timo gave the Witch Doctor a big, toothy smile. "Really?" he asked.

Melman nodded. "Go out there and grab life by the horns!" he urged his patient. Then Melman pulled off his gloves, the operation complete.

"Thank you, Dr. Mankoweicz!" Timo cheered.

Melman walked away from the operating rock, a few other giraffes following him to visit his next patient. "Break a leg!" he called back to Timo. Melman smiled, obviously enjoying his new job. "Sweet kid."

"Um . . ." Stephen said, clearing his throat. "That spot on your shoulder looks like Witch Doctor's Disease."

Melman chuckled. "That's the most ridiculous disease I've ever heard of, Stephen."

Then Melman saw his next patient. He stopped short. "Whoa," he said. It was an elephant with his trunk tied into a big bow knot.

"Don't ask," the elephant said glumly.

Melman examined the trunk. "Someone's been . . . knotty," he joked. Then he patted the elephant on the head. "This won't hurt a bit." He began pulling on the knot, wiggling the trunk.

A giraffe named Harland had overheard Stephen commenting on the brown spot on Melman's shoulder. "Joe, our last Witch Doctor . . ." Harland added. "He had a spot just like that."

"Mmm, mmm," Melman murmured, yanking on the elephant's knotted trunk.

"Yeah," Harland continued. "Monday . . . Joe. Wednesday . . . no Joe."

Melman stumbled backward as the snarl in the elephant's trunk came loose. "Wednesday . . . no Joe?" Melman repeated, regaining his balance.

"Ahh!" the elephant sighed. "I can breathe! Thanks, Doc!"

Melman faced the other giraffes, looking even more worried than usual. "So, this Witch Doctor's Disease is a real thing?"

They all nodded.

"You'll find a cure!" Stephen replied enthusiastically. "Hey, you've got at least forty-eight hours."

"But," Melman said, "I've never heard of it. What . . . um . . . I don't have any penicillin. I'm going to need a CAT scan just to get started!" Melman pressed his hoof against his chest to calm his frantically beating heart. "Sandy!" he called out.

An older female giraffe strode up to him.

She was wearing glasses and held a clipboard like a doctor's receptionist. "Mmm?" Sandy inquired.

"Cancel all my appointments," Melman said.

About a mile away from the valley, just a few feet from where the airplane had crashed, Skipper and Kowalski peered at a set of blueprints of the airplane redesign that Kowalski had drawn up.

Skipper turned the paper around, tracing lines with the tip of his flipper. "Looks impressive, Kowalski," he stated. "But will it fly?"

"Yes," Kowalski replied firmly. "If we fold it—" He grabbed the blueprints and creased the paper in a dozen places. "Here and here . . ." When he was done folding, he had a paper airplane. He tossed it, and it soared away.

"Nice," Skipper said.

The blueprint airplane flew toward the busy construction site where the building of the new, improved plane was already underway. Hundreds of monkeys and chimpanzees swarmed around the site, all hard at work helping Phil and Mason put the new flying machine together.

In the wreckage of the old plane, Alex sat in a passenger seat beside Marty. "I can't believe it," he moaned. He adjusted his fruity Hat of Shame on his head. "I've ruined my parents' lives."

"That is definitely not crack-a-lackin," Marty replied.

"No, it's *not* crack-a-lackin!" Alex agreed. "I've got to fix this! Maybe I should just go back to New York so my parents can have their life back."

Before the zebra could answer, Melman slunk onto the plane and took a seat behind Alex.

"Hey, Melman," Alex said.

Melman groaned and reached for a banana on Alex's hat. "There's something I gotta tell you."

Melman was interrupted by the arrival of

Gloria, who bustled into the plane wreckage with a big smile. "Hey, guys!" she greeted them. "Is this place great, or what?"

"I'd go with 'or what,'" Alex answered.

"Well, I'll tell you what," Gloria shot back. "You're not going to believe it, but . . . I've got a date with Moto Moto!"

Melman gulped. "Who's Moto Moto?" he squeaked.

Gloria fluttered her eyelashes. "Oh, he's so big and handsome," she replied. "And big. Do you know what 'Moto Moto' means?"

"It means 'Hot Hot,'" Marty answered.

"Hot Hot?" Melman muttered.

"Okay . . ." Gloria said, surprised by Marty's correct answer. "When did you start speaking African?"

"It's in my blood!" Marty responded.

Mason hopped into the plane wreckage and pointed to the seat Alex was sitting in. "Excuse me," the chimpanzee asked, "is this seat taken?"

"Um," Alex replied. "Actually, I'm kind of—"

"Thank you," Mason said, and he ripped the seat right out from under Alex and walked off with it.

"Don't worry," Melman snapped at Gloria, "you can flirt around with Mr. Hot Pants after I'm gone."

Gloria stared at the giraffe, confused by his attitude. "What's the deal, Melman?" she asked. "Why am I the parade and you're the rain?"

Melman sniffed. "Why do you have to drive your parade under my rain?"

"Maybe I'll just parade myself in another part of town!" Gloria bickered.

"Melman!" Alex scolded the giraffe. "Why don't you just tell her?"

"I don't know what you're talking about!" Melman screeched.

Gloria stuck her nose in the air. "So, I guess I'll go then."

"You know what?" Melman retorted. "Don't bother!" He jumped out of the plane wreckage and stormed away.

"Don't get up on my account!" Gloria

snapped, and she barreled off in the other direction.

Alex and Marty ran out of the wreckage, too. "Come back!" Alex called. "Melman! Gloria!"

"Hey," Marty said. "I thought you guys were friends."

"Come on, guys!" Alex shouted. "Marty is absolutely right!"

"Marty?" the zebra asked.

At that moment, another zebra arrived and asked the same question. "Marty?"

Alex stared at both zebras in shock. "Marty?" he repeated.

"What is going on here?" Marty asked.

Alex couldn't take his eyes off both zebras in front of him, bewildered by the similarity. "You're not . . . oh," he mumbled to the zebra he'd been talking to in the wreckage. He turned to the other zebra. "He was . . . no, I thought he . . . you're not him . . . oh."

"You thought that guy was me?" Marty demanded.

"No, no," Alex said quickly. "I mean . . . yes, yes. You guys do look . . . c'mon, really."

The first zebra snorted, offended. "You thought I was him?"

"You guys do kind of look a little . . ." Alex stammered. "Okay, you look a lot alike. You laugh alike, you talk alike . . . Marty, he has the same weird speech pattern as you do. It's a little weird, really. I mean, come on, Marty."

"So," Marty replied flatly, "you're saying there's nothing unique about me. I'm just like any other zebra."

"No!" Alex said. "Of course you're different!"

The two zebras stood next to each other. "How?" they both asked together.

Alex gaped at the zebras. He shook his head, flabbergasted. "Okay!" he cried. "I can't tell you apart! Maybe you could wear a bell or something. I don't know!"

"A bell?" Marty asked, sounding deeply hurt by the suggestion.

"Okay, not a bell," Alex said, back-tracking. "A bell's a bad idea."

"How about a T-shirt that says, 'I'm with stupid'?" Marty asked sarcastically.

"I'm not stupid," the other zebra said.

"Not you, stupid," Marty snapped. "*Him* stupid."

Alex put his hands on the sides of his head and groaned. "You know what?" he said. "I've been having pretty much the worst day of my life, okay?"

Marty shook his head. "It's always about you, isn't it, Alex?"

Alex pulled on his mane in frustration, squeezing his eyes shut. "Marty, could you give me a break?" When he opened his eyes, Marty was walking away. "Marty, don't turn your back on me."

But the real Marty was still standing next to him. "I'm right here," Marty said. "But you can't tell that, right?" With a final dirty look, Marty hurried to catch up to the other zebra. As he walked away, Marty called back over his shoulder, "Your 'one-in-a-million' friend hopes you enjoy your bigger-than-everyone-else's problems—alone!"

Alex slumped as he watched his best friend storm away. He'd never felt so miserable and alone in his life.

# 7

**W**ith the setting sun casting beautiful colors on the horizon, Julien and Maurice rode a pair of ostriches along the edge of the giraffe's dying hole area. The ostriches were followed by an entourage of flamingos.

Julien handled his ostrich masterfully. "Giddy up!" he cheered as he spurred the ostrich on.

Maurice wasn't as good at riding an ostrich. "Whoa!" he cried as the ostrich bumped him around. "Calm down!"

Julien pulled his ostrich up to a stop. "Look, Maurice," he said, gesturing at the landscape filled with giraffe dying holes and long neck bones everywhere. "Here's the perfect spot for my summer palace! So please fill in all these holes and relocate the riff-raff." Then Julien noticed Melman's head sticking out of one of the holes, lying flat on the ground despondently. "Oh," Julien said in distaste. "Who would leave a perfectly good head lying around?"

"What a waste," Maurice added.

Melman raised his head. "Tell me about it," he said sadly. "I'm in my prime here. I'm terminally ill, you know. I probably only have another two days left to live, tops."

"Ah, that's a bummer, man," said Maurice.

Julien sat up tall on his ostrich. "If I, King Julien, only had two days left to live, I would do all the things I've ever dreamed of doing!"

"Like what?" Melman asked.

"Oh," Julien replied, "I would love to learn how to whistle. I'm pretty good now, but I'd like to get better." He puckered up and blew out a lot of hot air. "You know what else I would do?" he continued. "I would invade a neighboring country and impose my own ideology even if they didn't want it."

Melman nodded. "That's easy for you to say," he told Julien. "You're a king."

"Yes," Julien agreed. "And you are only just an ugly little head. But there must be something you want to do before you die."

"Well . . ." Melman replied thoughtfully. "There is this one thing—"

"What is it?" Julien demanded. "Tell me!"

Melman let out a long sigh. "I never really had the guts to tell Gloria how I feel about her," he explained. "How I've always felt about her."

"Boring," Julien said. He started to ride off on his ostrich, but then he whirled around. "Oh! Is this Gloria a woman? You didn't tell me we were talking about a woman."

"What are you afraid of?" Maurice asked. "You're a dead man anyway."

"Yeah?" Melman wondered. "Yeah! You're right."

Julien leaned down off the ostrich, close to Melman's head. "Well, you're going to march right up to this woman, right?" he told the giraffe. "You look her right in the eye. And then you just tell her how much you hate her."

"Um," Melman replied. "Actually, it's more like 'love' her."

Julien cackled in glee. "Oh, you sly dog!" he hooted. "Woof woof! You are a real player! Now listen to me. You've got to rise up. You hearing me?"

"Yeah," Melman mumbled.

"I can't hear you!" Julien cried. He and Maurice started chanting "Rise up! Rise up!" until they inspired Melman to climb out of the hole.

"Go right up to her face!" Julien ordered. "And then you're going to say, 'Baby, I dig you!' Yeah!"

"Yeah!" Melman declared. "I'm going to do it!" He rushed off to find Gloria.

"Calm down," Julien sniped after the departing giraffe. "Nobody likes a show-off."

Over by the water hole, night had fallen, and Gloria and Moto Moto danced together in a romantic pool, staring up at the full moon above.

Moto Moto plucked a flower from the edge of the pool, and he began to pull off the petals slowly. "She loves me," the big hippo sang. "She loves my eyes. She loves me. She loves my thighs. She loves my roundness, she loves that I'm chunky. She loves that I'm plumpy. She loves me forever. She loves . . . because she loves me . . ."

Gloria giggled. "Moto Moto," she said, "before things get too serious . . . I was wondering if I were to, for example, stay here . . . I'd like to ask you—"

"Let your candied lips be the messengers to my ear canal," Moto Moto interrupted seductively.

Gloria blushed. "Well, I don't know," she said. "I have so many questions."

"I promise the answer will always be yes," said Moto Moto. "Unless 'no' is required."

"Okay," Gloria said. "So . . . what is it about me that you find so attractive?"

Moto Moto winked at her. "You are the most plumpin' girl I've ever met."

"Other than that," Gloria asked.

Genuinely surprised that his reply wasn't enough of an answer, Moto Moto thought hard about Gloria's question. "Let's see," he said. "Well, you know. You chunky."

Gloria squinted at him. "Right," she said.

"My gosh, girl," Moto Moto crowed. "You huge!"

"You've said that," Gloria replied, starting to sound annoyed.

"Yeah, that's right," said Moto Moto. "We don't have to talk no more." He leaned in for a kiss.

Before Moto Moto landed a smack on Gloria, Melman burst through the bushes around the pool. "Gloria!" he squealed. When

Melman saw that Gloria and Moto Moto were so close in the water, he slumped. "Gloria."

"Melman," Gloria said, surprised but happy to see the giraffe. "Melman, I want you to meet Moto Moto."

"Ah . . . Moto Moto," Melman said awkwardly. "Yeah, nice to meet you. Well, I, uh . . . I guess I . . . uh—"

Gloria smiled sweetly at Melman. "It's okay," she told him. "Apology accepted."

"Oh, yeah, right," Melman stammered. "Yes, that's why I . . . good." He let out a long breath. "Okay, well, that's it then." He turned to leave.

"Yeah, good," Moto Moto snapped. "We're kind of busy here, man."

Moto Moto's attitude froze Melman in place. "No, that's not it!" he snarled. Melman whirled around and grabbed a hunk of fat on Moto Moto's neck, pulling their faces close together. "Listen, Mototo," Melman growled. "You better treat this lady like a queen. Because you've found yourself the perfect woman. If I was ever so lucky to find the perfect woman, I would give her flowers every day! Her favorites are orchids—white orchids. And breakfast in bed! Six loaves of wheat toast, with butter on both sides! No crust! The way she likes it. I'd be her shoulder to cry on and her best friend. And I'd spend every day trying to think of how to make her laugh. She has the most amazing laugh. That's what I would do if I were you. But I'm not. So you do it."

Gloria gaped in shock at Melman as he let go of Moto Moto and rushed away through the bushes.

On the other side of the pool, a female hippo's head rose out of the water. "That was beautiful," she said, sniffling.

Moto Moto pushed the hippo back under. "Anyway, where were we?" he asked, turning to face Gloria.

Gloria gazed at the place where Melman had burst through the bushes, still blinking in amazement at the giraffe's heartfelt words.

"I'm huge," Gloria replied.

Meanwhile, Alex began training. He was still wearing his Hat of Shame.

"Oh, good morning. Surprised to see me, Makunga?" Alex punched at a bird's nest with a painted face on it. "You like that? This is for my dad!"

Just then a swarm of angry birds flew out of the nest and attacked him to the ground.

Alex coughed. "Who am I kidding?" he whimpered.

Alex heard a piercing scream echo through the valley. He ran to the edge of the cliff and peered down.

The water hole had gone dry.

"Oh, no," Alex said.

Down at the water hole, all the animals had gathered around the muddy, flat area where the water used to be. The scream had come from a fish flopping around in the mud. Now the fish was gasping in the air.

"The water," Stephen the giraffe fretted. "It's gone."

"Ooh," another giraffe said. "We're going to need a lot more dying holes."

All the animals muttered amongst themselves, frightened about the disappearance of all their water.

Makunga pushed through the crowd, followed by Teetsi. "Please, folks!" Makunga shouted. "Let me through." He stopped beside a dik-dik at the edge of the mud.

"The water hole dried up," the dik-dik told Makunga. The little animal pointed at a tiny puddle in the middle of the mud. "That's all that's left."

"Yes," Makunga said. "Good observation, Shirley."

"I'm Bobby," the dik-dik replied.

"What do we do, Makunga?" an elephant asked loudly.

"There isn't enough water for all of us!" a lioness yelled.

For a second, Makunga's face showed how worried he was, but then he forced himself to appear in control. "I'm afraid there is only one solution to this horrible crisis . . ."

"Fight for it!" Teetsi replied.

A terrified cry rose up from the animals at that idea.

"Fight for it?" a giraffe screeched.

"That's not fair," Bobby the dik-dik shouted. "You and Teetsi would win!"

Makunga raised his paws for silence. "Sorry, folks! But life isn't fair! Survival of the fittest."

Stephen stepped in front of the crowd. "Zuba would know what to do," he told the animals. "Where's Zuba?"

A general call for Zuba erupted among the animals.

"Hey!" Makunga roared, not liking that train of thought. "Zuba stepped down after being thoroughly disgraced by his pathetic excuse of a son. I'm in charge now—thanks to Alakay the Dancing Lion. Your best hope is to travel upriver and find out what happened to the water."

"Upriver?" an elephant trumpeted. "Off the reserve?"

"But no one leaves the reserve and survives!"

"Makunga has spoken!"

Alex looked at the dry riverbed and thought for a moment. He decided he had to be the one to travel upriver. He clenched his jaw and hurried across the savanna toward the border of the animal sanctuary. He had one stop to make first—the zebra grazing area in the tall grass near the border fence.

There were hundreds of identical zebras munching on the grass. Alex wandered through the throng, searching for Marty, but everyone around him looked the same.

"Marty?" Alex asked one zebra, who shook his head. Alex climbed onto a small hill and addressed the whole crowd. "Excuse me!" he called. "Zebras? Hi. Is Marty in there?"

Deep in the crowd, Marty lowered his head and turned his back to Alex.

The zebras started calling for Marty amongst themselves. "Marty? Has anyone seen Marty? Which one of us is Marty?"

Alex got no answer. He hung his head sadly. "All right," he said, giving up. "Well, if you see him, tell him his friend Alex came to say good-bye."

"Good-bye?" a zebra asked. "Where are you going?"

"Can we come?" another zebra wanted to know.

"No, no," Alex replied. "This is something I have to do alone." He walked over to the border and looked into the deep jungle on the other side. Then he took a deep breath and began to climb the fence.

"What are you doing?" a zebra screamed. "The hunters are out there!"

"Don't leave the reserve!" a bunch of zebras yelled together.

Alex looked one last time at the zebra herd. "Marty," he called out. "Look, I know you're in there. And before I go, I've got something I want to say. You've been a great friend. You've helped me so often to see the bright side of my problems that I never think of you as having any. What kind of friend does that make me?"

Alex let out a long breath. "A pretty lousy friend, I guess," he answered himself. "Well, I just want you to know that you're one in a million."

In the middle of the herd, Marty smiled halfheartedly at Alex's words.

"So," Alex continued, "could you please turn around, so I can tell you that to your face?"

Marty stiffened in surprise.

"That's right," Alex said. "I see you in there. Twelfth row. Two hundred third from the left. That's you, Marty. I know it's you. You know what makes you special? These guys, they're white with black stripes. You're black with white stripes. You're a dreamer, Marty . . . always have been. And you have great taste in music!"

That's what Marty wanted to hear. He hurried to the front of the herd. "Okay," he declared. "I'm in!"

Alex gazed happily at his best friend and pressed his paw against his chest to calm his thumping heart. But then Alex turned away and started climbing over the fence again. "No," he said firmly. "Marty, you can't come with me."

"You think you have a choice?" Marty

demanded. "But I've got to ask you . . . how did you know it was me? Really."

Marty hopped the fence and the two friends headed into the jungle.

"Marty, trust me," Alex explained. "I can look into your eyes and know it's you."

As they pushed their way through the underbrush, Alex glanced back quickly at Marty's butt.

It had a telltale scar of bite marks.

When Marty galloped up to the site of the plane crash, he was amazed to see that the redesigned plane was almost complete . . . but work on it had stopped. The chimpanzees were milling around in a big mob in front of the plane, holding up picket signs that read UNFAIR TO PRIMATES! and THE WORLD ISN'T BLACK AND WHITE! The chimps were on strike!

Marty pushed his way through the angry chimpanzees and found the penguins Skipper and Kowalski seated at a table across from the zoo chimps Mason and Phil. He hurried over to the table. "What's going on?" Marty demanded. "I need that plane for a rescue mission!"

"The plane won't be fixed until the suits meet our demands," Mason informed Marty. The chimp turned back to glare at Skipper. "Now," he said firmly, "about our maternity leave—"

"Maternity leave!" Skipper scoffed. "You're all males."

"Look," Marty broke in, "Alex is in big trouble!"

Skipper crossed his flippers over his chest. "Well, there's nothing I can do until we bust up this union."

Marty snorted in frustration. "I'm going to bust up all of you if you don't get this plane going!"

"Can't you see these commies have my hands tied here?" Skipper replied, gesturing at the striking chimps. He narrowed his eyes at Mason. "No maternity leave!"

Mason pulled out a slim manila envelope. He slid it across the table to Skipper.

Skipper opened the envelope and removed a few photos. The photos showed him kissing the dancing hula doll. Skipper blushed, and everyone around the table looked down at their feet, embarrassed for him.

"Maybe a certain someone wouldn't want these blowing around on the savanna," Mason said. "Hmm?"

Skipper slid the photos back into the envelope. He let out a long sigh. "All right," he conceded. "You get your maternity leave!"

"Finally!" Marty grunted.

Phil stood up on his chair and waved to the picketing chimpanzees, holding up his hands in a "V" for victory. The chimps all cheered and scrambled over to the plane, quickly banging it into shape.

Marty smiled. They'd be done in no time.

**8**

The frightened animals started digging deep wells around the water hole, hoping to hit water below the surface. So far, they hadn't had any luck, and they were all feeling tired, thirsty, and desperate.

Gloria waddled over to one of the wells and stuck her head down it. "Any water?"

She sat back as Moto Moto climbed up out of the well, holding an armful of glittering jewels. "No," he replied. "Just more diamonds and gold."

The crowd of animals groaned in disappointment as Moto Moto tossed the treasure onto the huge pile of rare gems they'd already collected.

"Okay," Gloria said, trying to sound uplifting. "Don't give up hope."

Moto Moto descended down the well again, returning to his digging.

"Attention, everybody!" Julien announced, arriving at the water hole on his ostrich. Behind him was Maurice on another ostrich, followed by a procession of flamingos and elephants. "There is only one way to get your precious water," Julien informed the crowd. "I, your beloved King Julien, must simply make a small sacrifice to my good friends, the water gods, in the volcano!"

The crowd murmured nervously, unsure that that was a good solution.

"What does that do?" a rhino asked.

"Listen, nincompoops," Julien said, "and I'll tell you. My sacrifice goes in the volcano, then the friendly gods eat up my sacrifice. They are grateful. They give me some of their water. Then I give it to you."

"What?" Gloria screeched.

"You know," Julien screeched back. "Science!"

"Does it work?" a dik-dik asked.

"No," Julien replied. "I mean, yes. Well . . ." He turned to look at the aye-aye on the ostrich behind him. "Maurice?"

"Eh," Maurice answered, shrugging. "Fifty-fifty."

All the animals stared at Julien for a long moment. He was talking about a crazy sacrifice. But without water . . .

"We'll do it!" all the creatures hollered together.

"Excellent," Julien said. "Now, all I need is someone who would like to go in the volcano and get eaten by gods. Any hands? Hands anybody?"

The zebras immediately bolted from the

crowd, swiftly disappearing around a hill.

The other animals shifted nervously, looking around at each other. Nobody volunteered. Moto Moto ducked down into the well, hiding from view.

"Come on!" Julien demanded. "It's not like they're going to eat you!" He stopped and reconsidered, petting his ostrich. "Sorry; I mean, it's like they're going to eat you. Okay . . . I need someone, perhaps someone who has never found love, who could look death straight in the eyeball. A real massive—"

Melman popped out of some nearby bushes. "I'll do it," he said.

"Melman?" Gloria cried.

All the animals cheered. They rushed toward Melman and hoisted him up on their shoulders, draping him with flower garlands. Then they started carrying him toward the distant volcano. "Sacrifice!" they shouted.

Atop his ostrich, Julien laughed hysterically. "We have our volunteer!"

Gloria hurried over to Melman's side. "Melman," she called up to him as she ran alongside the crowd. "What is wrong with you?"

"I'm dying anyway," Melman replied. "If it will get you water, it'll be worth it."

"Are you nuts?" Gloria bawled.

Melman shook his head. "Gloria, I just want you to know," he said, "back at the zoo, it was never the doctors or the prescriptions that kept me going. It was always you. Seeing you every day. That's what kept me going!"

The crowd surged around Melman, pushing Gloria away from him. She fell behind the procession of animals.

"Melman!" she shouted. "Wait!"

Meanwhile, deep in the jungle, Marty and Alex hiked up the dry riverbed toward the source of the water. Alex was convinced it would be as easy to fix as a clogged pipe.

"Look, Marty," Alex explained, "if we get the water back, maybe my dad will think I'm . . . I just want to show I'm a real lion."

"As opposed to a chocolate lion?" Marty joked.

Alex shook his head. "I know this might

sound hard to believe, but, apparently, lions don't dance."

Marty gasped. "What!?"

"At least as far as my dad is concerned."

"As far as the people were concerned, you were a huge hit."

"Thanks, Marty," responded Alex. "But that was New York. This is Africa. It's a much tougher crowd."

As they climbed the riverbank over a rise, a vast dam appeared up the river in front of them, looming over the jungle like an ancient wooden temple.

Alex stopped in his tracks. "This is the clog!" he exclaimed, and he let out a long whistle.

They hurried the rest of the way up the riverbed toward the dam. From the top, they saw Nana's sprawling camp filled with tourists.

"We're going to need more manpower," Alex said.

"Let's get your dad," Marty suggested.

Alex raised his eyebrows. "I was thinking of the penguins."

"Of course," Marty replied.

They both cringed when they heard the sharp report of a rifle, and Alex's Hat of Shame exploded on his head in a burst of blasted fruit.

Marty and Alex whirled around to see a hunting party of people charging out of the jungle underbrush. The people waved spears at them.

"Savages!" Marty yelled.

"Evasive maneuvers!" Alex screamed.

They took off running down the riverbed. The savages chased them, hurling their spears.

Alex and Marty didn't run in a straight line. To avoid the spears and arrows—or gunshots—they ran in strange patterns down the hill. "Serpentine!" Marty cried, weaving as he fled. "Zigzag!"

"Squiggly!" Alex hollered as the missiles barely missed him. "Squiggly-squid! No, octopus!"

"Zigzag!" Marty screamed back, ducking under a chucked spear.

Booby traps exploded around them as

they barreled their wiggly way down the dry river. Alex screamed as a rope snare snagged his leg, hoisting him into the air. He dangled upside down above Marty.

"Alex!" Marty wailed.

"Run, Marty!" Alex yelled.

*Thonk!* A spear embedded itself in a tree trunk right next to Marty's head.

"Come on," Marty called. "I can't leave you here!"

Then a huge log studded with spikes swung down toward Marty. He narrowly missed it by dodging to the left. Marty realized he couldn't stay there any longer—the hunters were getting closer, and were still throwing spears.

"Go!" Alex hollered. "Get help! Squiggly-squid maneuver!"

"I'll be back!" Marty cried. He took off down the riverbed, weaving randomly as he ran.

Marty disappeared around a bend, hidden by the jungle, just as the hunters appeared under Alex.

"Let me go, please! Come on. This must be some sort of misunderstanding!" Alex pleaded.

The people ignored him as the hunting party placed Alex on a spit over an unlit fire pit. Alex recognized the people now as the tourists Nana had been with in the truck. They looked very hungry.

"Now, how about a nice lion casserole?" Nana cheered as she grabbed a torch to light the fire.


Back at the water hole, a panicked zebra ran into Makunga.

"Makunga! Alakay and Marty left the reserve, heading upriver!"

"Oh no, this is horrible," Makunga sneered.

"You gotta do something" exclaimed the zebra.

"Don't worry, I know exactly what to do."

He traveled to Zuba.

"Zuba! Zuba . . ." cried Makunga.

"Get out of here," ordered Zuba.

Zuba started to advance on Makunga but Florrie stopped him.

"What do you want, Makunga?" she asked warily.

"It's awful! The water hole dried up!" Makunga whined.

"Well, you're the Alpha Lion, Makunga, what are you going to do about it?" roared Zuba.

"Your son, Alakay, said he could fix it. He's gone upriver."

"No!" Alex's parents both yelped.

"I tried to stop him. But he was determined to prove himself to you," chuckled Makunga.

"Hurry Zuba!" pleaded Florrie.

Zuba sprinted off to save his son.

Meanwhile, the animal procession reached the top of the volcano. They spread out around the rim and lowered Melman onto a long ledge that stretched out over the smoking caldera filled with molten lava. A lion beat on a big drum, the bass note echoing rhythmically across the crater.

Taking a deep breath, and wrinkling his nose at the sulfurous fumes, Melman started inching out onto the ledge. "Okay, okay," he muttered nervously.

"Jump!" the animals chanted. "Jump!"

"Okay, here we go," Melman said as he reached the edge.

"*JUMP!*" all the animals hollered.

"All right, already!" Melman shot back. "Don't rush me." He gulped and got into position on the edge, preparing to dive into the lava below.

At the back of the crowd, Gloria tried to shove her way toward Melman, but she couldn't get through. "Melman!" she screamed, elbowing a rhino in front of her. "Move out of the way!" She spotted Julien off to the side and plowed through the animals toward him. "Julien, stop this!" she pleaded. "This is crazy!"

"Oh," Julien scoffed. "Suddenly throwing a giraffe into a volcano to make water is crazy!"

"Yes!" Gloria replied.

"Throw him in and prove it, then," Julien suggested.

Gloria rolled her eyes and barreled through the crowd until she reached the entrance to the long ledge over the volcano. Melman raised his arms, about to dive. "Melman, stop!" Gloria screeched.

Melman turned around and blinked at her. "Gloria?"

"You can't do this!" Gloria insisted.

Melman shrugged. "Why not?"

"Because—" Gloria began, but she slipped on the sheer ledge and fell to her knees.

The rock ledge couldn't bear the weight of her hippopotamus body. It crumbled under Melman's hooves.

Melman tried to scramble up the collapsing ledge, but he plummeted toward the lava.

Quick as a blink, Gloria reached out and snagged the top of Melman's neck. He dangled from her grip, suspended high above the molten rock.

The animals around the crater rim gasped

at the bizarre sight of a hippo holding a giraffe above a volcano.

"You can't do this, Melman," Gloria said firmly.

"First of all," Melman replied, pointing at his neck, "that hurts. Second of all, I've only got eighteen hours to live anyway."

"Melman, I've got to know," Gloria asked. "Did you really mean all those things you said about me?"

"Of course I did," Melman answered.

Gloria sighed. "It's crazy," she said.

Melman's brow furrowed. "It is?"

Gloria yanked Melman up and deposited him safely next to her on the volcano's rim. "Yes," she said. "It's crazy to think that I had to go halfway around the world to find out that the perfect guy for me lived right next door."

Melman searched her eyes to make sure she was serious. She was. His face lit up in a giant grin. "Then I guess it's you and me, neighbor," he said happily. "For the next . . . eighteen hours."

"I'll take whatever I can get," Gloria replied, squeezing him in a big hug.

Julien ran over, waving his arms. "Whoa!" he cried. "Maurice, what just happened?"

Maurice smiled. "I believe the fat lady has sung," he said.

An out-of-breath zebra appeared in the crowd. "Hey, what's going on?" he huffed.

"Marty!" exclaimed Gloria.

"Would you just jump into the volcano already. We're thirsty over here!"

Just then another zebra, the real Marty, appeared.

"Get the heck out of here!" he demanded as he shoved the imposter away.

"Hey, listen up. Alex is in trouble and we have to get upriver fast."

"What about the plane!" Melman exclaimed.

# 9

"**C**ome on, folks. I'm really not good for BBQ—too tough and chewy!" Alex begged just as a human jammed an apple into his mouth.

Suddenly a deep growl bellowed throughout the camp.

"Lion!" yelled a human.

Alex spit out the apple. "Dad!" he cried.

Zuba charged toward the campfire, roaring. With a powerful leap, he knocked Alex away from harm.

"Don't let them get away!" Nana ordered.

Screaming, the tourists surrounded Alex and Zuba.

"What were you thinking?" Zuba demanded angrily as he clawed the vines binding Alex. "You've got no business being out here."

The wild-looking tourists, armed with spears and bows and arrows, surrounded the two lions and warily started stepping closer.

Zuba dropped down in a fighting stance. "This is it," he told Alex. "Stay behind me. I want you to run for it while I attack."

Alex put his paw on Zuba's shoulder. "No, Dad," he said. "I can handle these guys. They're just rude and frightened New Yorkers."

Zuba shoved Alex behind him. "I said stay back!" he snarled.

Extending his claws, Zuba prepared to pounce.

Wide eyed, Alex took in the whole situation—his father was about to fight armed people, and it was going to be bloody. He suddenly knew what he had to do.

A second before Zuba clashed with the tourists, Alex leaped in front of his father.

He started to dance.

Alex stuck his arms up in a dramatic pose and pirouetted, then threw his head back as he jumped up on his toes.

The tourists froze in place, dumbfounded by the dancing lion.

"What are you doing, Son?" Zuba demanded.

Alex shimmied in front of the hunters. "The only thing I know how to do!" He boogied and pranced, shaking his stuff.

One male tourist scratched his head. "Hey," he said, "I know those moves. Is that . . . Alex?"

As Alex continued to dance, the tourists lowered their spears one by one.

"It's Alex the Lion!" a woman called out. "From the New York Zoo!"

"But he was lost at sea," another tourist added. "I saw it in the paper."

A bedraggled woman put her hands on her hips. "It's got to be him," she said.

Alex didn't pause in his dance routine. He kicked and wiggled, and tap danced a fast section.

The tourists cheered in awe. "Alex! Alex! Alex!"

Zuba stared at his son, stunned with pride. He started to bob to Alex's rhythm, and before he knew it, he was dancing, too!

Zuba hopped into the dance beside Alex. He wasn't an experienced dancer, but he was surprisingly talented. "I don't know what I'm doing," he said nervously.

"Just do what I do," Alex instructed. "Don't worry, Dad." He reached out and touched Zuba's birthmark on his paw. "You were born with it!"

Then Alex leaped into the air, fluttering his paws above his head, and Zuba copied him.

"Is this right, Son?" Zuba asked, fluttering his arms.

"Don't think, Dad," Alex replied. "*Feel!* Be the butterfly."

Zuba followed Alex's lead as they spun together in front of the savage tourists. Then they leaped up together and landed with a final flourish, dropping into Alex's famous final pose. Together they let out an ear-splitting roar.

The tourists erupted in cheers, clapping loudly for the famous lion.

Zuba started to laugh. "My son!" he cried. "The King of New York!"

Still grinning, Alex bowed deeply to his audience, and they cheered even louder. Loving the attention, Alex couldn't stop smiling.

But then his smile vanished when he saw Nana pushing through the crowd.

"What kind of dinner theatre is this?" she howled.

In the instant before Nana charged the two lions, a big metal barrel dropped down in front of her.

Alex gaped at the barrel dangling in the air in front of him, and as Alex looked up, he could see that it was held in place by a long chain of linked chimpanzees, who were hanging out of an incredible propeller plane hovering above the camp.

The crowd gasped, shocked by the airplane's arrival.

Marty stuck his head out of the plane's bay door. "Alex!" he shouted. "Get in!"

"Get us to safety, then we'll go back for the dam!" Alex yelled.

"What?!" Marty called back.

"He said, 'We've got to be hasty. Use us as a battering ram,'" responded Mason.

"Skipper!" yelled Marty. "I think Alex wants to take out the dam!"

"All right," said Skipper. "But it's his funeral."

Alex and Zuba leaped into the barrel. The chimps strained to hold on, peering down at the lions. The plane's propeller roared louder as it lifted the lions above the camp.

Nana had moved to the top of the dam and was waving her arms with fury. "That's our dinner!" she hollered.

The plane swung around in the sky, turning toward the dam. "Rico!" Skipper ordered. "Full throttle!"

Rico pulled a lever on the dashboard. Back in the fuselage, bunches of bananas dropped in front of dozens of chimps who were straining to turn the cranks that powered the plane's propeller. When they saw the bananas, the chimps cranked faster, and the plane zoomed toward the dam.

"I'll show you hooligans!" Nana bawled, swinging her fists back and forth at the plane.

Peeking over the edge of the barrel, Alex saw that they were swinging directly toward the dam's giant logs. His eyes popped wide. "Tell them no!" he yelled at the nearest chimp. "Pull up! They'll kill us! There's got to be another way! Pass it on."

The message zipped chimp to chimp up the chain. At the top, Mason once again translated for Marty. "They say, 'No pull up. Kill us! There's no other way. Basset hound!'"

"Are you sure?" Marty asked skeptically.

"Let's do this!" Skipper announced. "There is no sacrifice greater . . . than someone else's."

"Hold on!" Alex screamed.

*BA-BOOM!*

The big metal barrel plowed right through the logs on top of the dam, splintering some and knocking the others loose.

All along its length, the dam rumbled, and then crumbled, toppling down. Gushes of water spewed over the falling logs.

# 10

At the water hole, Makunga lifted a leaf cup full of liquid to his mouth while the other animals stared on, their tongues hanging out of their mouths. Suddenly, a rumble thundered throughout the ground. Makunga turned his head to figure out what caused the noise just in time to be engulfed by a giant wave. The water hole filled with refreshing, clean, life-giving water as Zuba and Alex rode their barrel to shore. The animals erupted with glee.

"It's a miracle!" cried a dik-dik.

"They brought the water back!" praised a giraffe.

"My son! He saved us all!!" boasted Zuba, getting to his feet.

The animals continued their cheering as Alex hugged his mother and father tightly.

"Hey! Quiet! Silence!" growled Makunga, staggering out of the water.

Makunga glanced calmly between Zuba and Alex. "If I remember correctly," he told Zuba, "you quit the pride." He glared at Alex. "And you were kicked out. So, technically speaking, neither one of you can challenge me."

Alex laughed. "We are not going to challenge you. In fact, we humbly present you with this token of appreciation for, in a way, bringing us together," he said. Makunga looked stunned as Alex presented him with a purse.

"I don't know what to say," Makunga said, baffled.

"It's a man bag. Very popular where I come from."

Makunga nodded with interest and tried the bag on over his shoulder. "I accept your tribute. But I'm afraid you're still banished," Makunga declared.

"We figured you'd say that," said Alex as he and his father tipped over the barrel, releasing Nana. She rolled out, slowly rose to her feet, and squinted at the lion carrying her purse.

"Bad kitty!" she cried. Nana kicked Makunga solidly in the groin.

"Ah! No! Ow! Agh!" Makunga screeched, falling to the ground and dropping his scepter. He struggled back to his paws, and Nana chased him down the path.

Alex picked up the fallen scepter. He stared at the staff for a second, then smiled and handed it over to Zuba.

Zuba returned Alex's smile. He raised the

scepter high in the air. "Hey, everyone!" Zuba announced. "Drinks are on me!"

The crowd let loose a wild cheer and leaped into the water. The celebrations lasted well into the night.